WITHDRAWN

# RIDE THE STORM

# RIDE THE STORM

BY

EMMA DARCY

MILLS & BOON LIMITED
ETON HOUSE   18–24 PARADISE ROAD
RICHMOND   SURREY   TW9 1SR

First published in Great Britain 1992
by Mills & Boon Limited

© Emma Darcy 1992

Australian copyright 1992
Philippine copyright 1992
Large Print edition 1993

ISBN 0 263 13315 X

Set in Times Roman 16 on 17 pt.
16-9303-56069 C

Printed and bound in Great Britain by
William Clowes, Beccles, Suffolk.

# CHAPTER ONE

IT WAS ALMOST MIDNIGHT when they rounded the headland. Garret turned the old fishing trawler toward the marina at Leisure Island. *We're right on schedule,* Tiffany thought, trying to calm a sudden jangle of nerves as she anxiously scanned the fleet of millionaires' yachts berthed at the exclusive resort.

She had picked the hour deliberately. It was late enough to be unlikely that many people would be drifting around the marina, and those who were would hardly stop to question why a fishing trawler should be passing by. But it was not too late to be arriving at a party. Not the kind of party Joel Faber gave for his jet-set friends.

It was not difficult to pick out his yacht. There had been many photographs of it featured in both newspapers and magazines— the most luxurious ever designed and built for an Australian businessman.

"There!" Tiffany pointed triumphantly.

"Aye. *Liberty* it is!" There was a sting of acid scorn in Garret's naming of the yacht. "He'd get no feel of the sea in that boat."

The old fisherman had been working the sea all his life. Clearly he had little respect for those who played on it. Nevertheless he steered the old trawler toward *Liberty,* apparently wanting a closer look at the super yacht before getting down to the serious task of dropping off Tiffany at the most inconspicuous place.

The sound of music drifted across the water. The party on board was in full swing, just as Tiffany had expected it to be by this time. Her plan to gate-crash it was a wild gamble, she knew, but if only she could get to Joel Faber she was reasonably confident of persuading him to at least listen to her. And that was half the battle. The whole battle up to this point! Just to get him to listen!

Months of frustrated efforts had finally led her to this approach by stealth. Tiffany was not used to being beaten. At twenty-eight years of age she had enough worldly experience under her belt to feel confident of achieving almost anything, yet all her ingenuity and skill at handling people had not

effected a meeting with Joel Faber through
any normal channels. She had been compre-
hensively blocked at every turn. But Tiffany
wouldn't admit defeat, not when it meant
defeat to those near and dear to her.

"More security guards," Garret barked, his
eyes trained on the jetty where two men stood
at the bottom of the gangplank that led on to
the yacht. "They're not there for the purpose
of sniffing the night air. This is a useless task.
We might as well turn around and go home."

"No!" Tiffany cried in instinctive protest,
even though her heart sank at this last un-
anticipated obstacle to her quest.

"You won't get past them, girl. Joel Faber
has got you beaten again."

"Not yet," she returned stubbornly. *I have
to try,* she added to herself. Come hell or high
water she was going to reach Joel Faber tonight. "I will get past them," she insisted.

She would lie her way past them, or create
some kind of scene or diversion that would
win her way into the party. One way or
another, whatever it took, she would do it.
Joel Faber was their best chance—probably
their only chance—of getting the help and

support they needed. The end result would make every bit of trouble worthwhile.

"It won't work anyway," old Garret muttered pessimistically. "The devil will take him first."

Tiffany shot him a searching look. "Why do you say that?"

Garret instantly closed up, just as all the old-timers at Haven Bay did when Joel Faber's name was mentioned. He was the most famous person ever to come from the old fishing village, yet no one wanted to talk about him. They were all pessimistic about Tiffany's chances of arranging a deal with him.

Tiffany figured they were jealous of his success, or perhaps resented the fact that he had left Haven Bay behind and made good elsewhere. Or maybe they thought of him as some kind of deserter for walking away from everything after "the storm".

That "storm" twenty years ago was still a bitter memory. So many lives had been lost, Joel Faber's grandfather among them. After that tragedy, and with no other family to keep him there, Tiffany thought it perfectly natural that the sixteen-year-old boy leave and look for another kind of life. No one could reasonably blame him for that.

And yet, Tiffany sometimes had the disquieting feeling there was something else— something that wasn't being told. She had always shrugged it off as being fanciful nonsense. Garret McKeogh was looked up to as a leader in Haven Bay and he had supported Tiffany's ideas for revitalising the village from the very start, agreeing that Joel Faber was the best man to approach for help. He hadn't wavered in that judgement anywhere along the line, even going so far as cooperating with tonight's scheme.

So why did he seem to be denying her any chance of success now? And the way he had spoken, with that hard edge to his voice . . . it was almost as though he hated Joel Faber. It made Tiffany wonder if she had been deceived in some way.

She grew impatient with Garret's silence. "What don't I know, Garret?" she asked sharply. "What is it that you haven't told me? Why won't it work?"

His weather-beaten face gave nothing away. The grizzled grey beard made him look like some Old Testament figure of authority and

zeal and rectitude. The steel-grey eyes seemed
fixed on some far distance. But his gnarled
old hands caressed the steering wheel
indecisively.

"I wasn't counting on more guards," he
said at last. "Coming by sea, I thought we'd
be inside all his fancy security, just the way
we planned. Now it won't work. I don't want
you to get arrested for trespassing, Tiffany.
That's carrying it too far."

Even if things went wrong, she could hardly
be put into gaol for such a little piece of
trickery, Tiffany reasoned. It wasn't grand
fraud or anything like that. More than likely
she would be considered a nuisance and
warned off—if she were caught.

"It's still worth a try," she insisted.
"Nothing too bad can happen."

Garret's fingers clenched and unclenched
as the steel-grey eyes bored at her, through
her, as if he were seeing something else behind
her. "You have a good heart, Tiffany James.
A giving heart. As have all your family. I
don't want you to get hurt. Not in any way
at all."

"I'm not a child, Garret," she returned
firmly. "I can look after myself. As for my

family, you know how disappointed Carol and Alan will be if I go home empty-handed again. For their sakes, I have to take this chance.''

She knew Garret was fond of Alan. Tiffany couldn't think of anyone at Haven Bay who didn't care about her sister's son at least to some degree, if only out of admiration for the way he rose above the difficulties that life had handed him.

Alan deserved the kind of future he wanted for himself, and Tiffany was bent on doing her level best to make it possible. She wanted to take the look of strain and worry out of Carol's eyes, and see the sparkle of light and life that should be there. Her sister had sacrificed so much for her son's sake. It was well past time that someone lightened the burden of the future.

Their foster parents had taught them that was what family was for—sharing loads, helping one another, standing shoulder to shoulder against any adversity. All of Tiffany's brothers and sisters had tried to meet one another's needs as a matter of course, whenever it was possible, and Tiffany was in the best position to help this time. It was up to her. And if she got Joel Faber's backing for her project, the problem of the future would very definitely be solved.

"So be it then," Garret finally agreed, his face setting with grim purpose. "I hope you get to him."

Tiffany sighed her relief in his reaffirmation of co-operation. The old man was worried about her. That was all. Any animosity he had towards Joel Faber was undoubtedly inspired by the man's security measures.

"Thank you, Garret," she said with an appeasing smile.

He flashed her a dark look. "Not that I think you will."

"That's up to me," she retorted quickly and turned back to the marina, intent on action and no further argument. "The pier at the far end..." She pointed. "I'll make my way from there."

Without another word Garret swung the wheel to bring the boat around to the best line of approach.

Tiffany started to rehearse in her mind the part she would play. It was only a matter of confidence, she told herself. The expensive

white outfit she was wearing was classy
enough to suggest she was at home in élite
society. Her hairstyle was straight out of a
fashion magazine. On looks alone, she was
certain she could pass as a guest. All she
needed was a little piece of luck on her side.
She had never yet failed to get out of any
sticky situation when the occasion demanded
some quick-witted thinking and fast action.

So she had nothing to worry about.

Nothing at all.

One way or another she *would* get to Joel
Faber and make him listen to her.

# CHAPTER TWO

JOEL FABER STOOD on the rear deck of his yacht, his back turned to the partying guests and the general revelry. His mind was tired of making the kind of conversation expected of him. He wanted a quiet breathing space from the pumped-up atmosphere that had pervaded the past few hectic days and was especially prevalent tonight—people hanging on to the excitement with almost feverish tenacity, as if it might never be this good again.

It was a soft balmy night, perfect, and everything he had planned had been brought to a perfect culmination. Leisure Island—the newest and most exclusive housing estate in Australia—had been launched with the kind of glittering celebration that befitted its status, and there was nothing left for him to do—except see out the night. And keep raking in the profits.

Joel knew he should be savouring the sweet taste of success. He should, at least privately, be exulting over the doubters who had warned

14

him he was going in too big, that the market he was aiming at was too small, and that he would end up with a white elephant that would bleed him dry and leave him bankrupt. But all he felt towards those men now was pity and a faint contempt. Success was almost too easy to be really sweet any more.

What he did feel—and his mouth stretched into a thin self-mocking smile as he silently acknowledged the truth—was only a flat sense of emptiness. The same sense of emptiness he had felt all these years. Even more so now that all his ambitions were fulfilled. There was nothing else to do, nothing of any moment to achieve.

He had poured the past two years of his life into this project, turning what had been virtually a swamp into something beautiful. The luxury environment would of course appeal to the very rich: top-class golf course, marina, waterfront homes with private jetties, a five-star international hotel and shopping complex that boasted the best of everything; and with the causeway linking the island with the mainland it was all within easy driving distance of Surfers' Paradise and Brisbane. The Gold Coast of Queensland really was the Gold

Coast, Joel thought with cynical appreciation. The money just kept rolling in. Like the ocean. Endless waves of it. And he should be riding high instead of feeling flat and empty.

Perhaps it was because there weren't any real risks left in his life any more. His drive and the business know-how he had acquired were enough to guarantee success in any venture. He had been in the real estate game too long not to recognise what would go and what wouldn't.

What he needed was a storm in his life. Even now, after all these years, the turbulent clash of nature's elements gave him physical disquiet . . . a restless brooding uneasiness. He would never forget. Not on one level of consciousness. On another pragmatic level, he had to forget in order to achieve the will and purpose to go forward. There was no way to go back, no way to make the past different, no way to change what had happened. If he had been granted a choice back then, he would have given his life. The only option left had been to keep forging ahead, to keep . . . forgetting.

There were other risks to take. If they didn't work out, at least they sparked his interest for a while. Like Q2RV. Buying that television station had seemed a smart idea at the time, but he was pouring good money after bad there. Better to off-load it and invest in something more profitable... more personally rewarding.

Irritated at having let his mind drift back to business, he turned around, leaned back against the railing and slowly swept his gaze around the beautiful people he had invited on board as a follow-up to the star-studded concert that had marked the grand opening of the hotel. The cast of characters was a yardstick of his own elevated status, but even that didn't mean much any more. He had met royalty, been accepted by the establishment, mixed with all the high rollers and moved as an equal among the other risk takers who made money work for them. It had all meant something once. And of course it still did. It simply didn't mean all that much any more.

He felt distanced from it tonight, as if he had been there and done that and moved beyond it. Yet what was beyond it? He shook his head and tried to focus his mind on some-

thing more tangible. It seemed absurd that he
had to work at enjoying his own party. The
thing to do was relax and let the night bring
its own pleasures. It was all that was left to
him really.

A woman—that was what he needed.
Someone to distract him, amuse him, pleasure
him. He hadn't bothered with a replacement
for Nanette since she had left on her mar-
keting trip to Europe. He'd been too busy
with the project and too uninterested. But
perhaps tonight...

His gaze lingered on the rich burgundy
mane that was Germaine's trademark in the
modelling world—beautiful hair, soft, silky,
sexy—and she tossed it with pointed effect
when her eyes caught his in sharp speculation. He smiled a brief acknowledgment.
But the party was still young and he was not
ready to encourage Germaine yet. He might
prefer someone else.

With inoffensive casualness he slid his gaze
away, cynically amused at his own arrogance,
but all too aware that there wasn't a single
woman here that he couldn't have. And if he
were inclined to adultery, which he wasn't,
quite a few married ones as well. But no

woman had ever meant so much to him that
he invited that kind of trouble upon himself,
although it was easy enough to recognise the
availability in their eyes. Once it had excited
him, pleased him. It was a measure of his
worth in the world. And for a boy who had
come from being regarded as the lowest of the
low, every bit of esteem meant something.

Even now, although he viewed the situation
far more objectively, he had no objection to
being wanted by women. Wealth, prestige,
power...women recognised those values. That
they wanted him was an index of his success.
But he didn't intend being used. Wanting was
one thing, marriage quite another. Joel had
been alone far too long to see marriage as
anything other than a confinement he
wouldn't like. He now had the kind of
freedom he had dreamed of as a boy. He had
worked for it. He owed nobody anything.
And he wanted to keep it that way.

Nevertheless, he was no monk and he saw
no reason to reject what was freely offered.
So freely that the degree of effort required
from him was getting smaller and smaller all
the time. Not that he had ever been hard-
pressed to attract a woman, but now he

doubted it would matter if he were as ugly as sin and twice his present age. Wealth was a powerful aphrodisiac. The fact that he was only thirty-six years old and in the prime of his manhood added to his desirability.

He deplored his own cynicism, aware that it was growing like a disease inside him, gobbling up the ideals he had once nursed. But the implacable truth was that there wasn't much that could be done about it. Most of the people he encountered were totally selfish, interested only in their own egos and self-advancement. That was the problem. And always would be.

He had thought it would be different when he left his childhood behind, when he became rich and successful; but the more things changed, the more they stayed the same. He could draw any number of people around him any time he liked now, but who would stay if he were bankrupted tomorrow? He had to be self-sufficient to survive. "Sink or swim," his grandfather told him long ago, and no one would offer a helping hand now any more than old Reuben had then.

With an impatient sigh at these morose thoughts, Joel stared out over the marina and caught sight of the boat approaching. It was coming in without any lights, which instantly piqued his curiosity. The full moon allowed him to make out the distinctive lines of a fishing trawler. He had seen plenty of them in his time. It was out of place here, and he wondered what it was doing.

The engines suddenly slowed. It chugged quietly toward a pier some hundred yards away from *Liberty*'s berth. It was impossible to say it stopped. There was a momentary pause, a flash of light in the darkness, then with effortless expertise the motors opened up, the nose of the boat snubbed about, and it was off down the bay and fast disappearing.

Joel frowned at the diminishing transom of the trawler. He felt no prickle of danger, no uneasy premonition. Nevertheless, the whole incident was unusual and it portended something. His eyes scanned the pier. He saw nothing moving. He switched his gaze to the foreshore and there she was—a woman in white—emerging from the darkness and relatively unnoticeable as she moved past the line of yachts.

That she had jumped off the trawler Joel had no doubt whatsoever. It was one way of avoiding the security checkpoint on the causeway, which protected all Leisure Island guests from the intrusion of undesirables. Security was one of the attractions for wealthy people, and tonight it was especially tight. Only concert-ticket holders, hotel guests, homeowners and people who had been privately invited had any right to be here. Exclusivity was another attraction.

Joel wondered what purpose the woman had in mind. He decided that if she changed direction and moved out of sight he would alert his own security guards, who were posted at the bottom of the gangplank that led from the jetty to the deck of *Liberty*. Burglary did not fit into the scheme for Leisure Island. In the meantime the woman was only trespassing, and it was interesting to watch her.

When she stepped on to his jetty, Joel's interest was immeasurably heightened. There was nothing spectacular about her but she certainly had style. She exuded an air of determined purpose as she walked with long-legged grace toward the security men. Her tapered trousers accentuated the lithe feminine curve of hip and thigh, and a body-hugging vest made the most of her small waist and full sculptured breasts. One hand was hooked under the collar of a matching jacket that was casually slung over her shoulder. She carried a small glittery evening bag in her other hand.

Her hair was a light honey-brown, long and straight except for the slight curl where it swirled around her shoulders. There was a feathery sort of fringe near the side parting that no doubt helped to keep her hair from falling over her face. It was an attractive face: large darkly fringed eyes, straight nose, generous mouth, firm chin held proudly above a long graceful neck. The kind of neck that invited jewellery. Yet she wore none. And the only discernible make-up she had used was a soft coral lipstick.

She was, of course, a total stranger. Joel knew he had never seen her before in his life. And he hadn't invited any strangers to this party. Nevertheless, she approached the security men with nonchalant confidence. He watched, intrigued to see how she would handle herself.

TIFFANY'S HEART was hammering in her throat. She didn't know if the guards had a

guest list from which they checked off names,
or what the procedure was for getting past
them, but obviously they weren't standing
there for nothing. She would have to play the
whole thing by ear. The important thing was
to look as if she had every right to be here
and act accordingly.

The men were watching her approach.
There didn't seem to be any doubtful questions on their faces. They held nothing in their
hands. For one wild moment, Tiffany thought
she might be able to walk straight between
them and on to the yacht, but that hope was
abruptly dashed when she was just a couple
of steps short of them.

"Good evening, ma'am. Your invitation?"

"It is a grand evening, isn't it?" she tem-
porised, sweeping an appreciative gaze to the
full moon and the star-studded sky while her
mind whirled with frantic invention. How
could she produce an invitation when she
didn't have one? Would they accept that she
had lost it? No, too risky. They might want
to check her name then. She had to make
them believe she had an invitation.

She flashed a winning smile at the man who
had spoken, opened her evening bag, started

to put her hand in, then rolled up her eyes in a look of exasperated recollection. ''I left it on the bar table of the Bentley. I meant to put it in my bag, but I put it down while I poured myself a drink and...''

She swung around to look back down the jetty. ''Payton's already driven off to park. Which is a problem!'' She expelled a long sigh, gave the guard a look of appeal that apologetically begged his indulgence, then pitched her voice to a tone that expected it. ''It isn't really necessary, is it? I'd have to walk over to the hotel, find Payton, find the Bentley...''

The security man regretfully shook his head. ''I'm sorry, ma'am. I can't let you—''

''I know!'' she cut in brightly, then injected an imperious note, hoping she sounded like the pampered rich girl she had just conjured up. ''You can get it for me! Would you be kind enough to save me the bother? Just go over to the hotel and page Payton. No doubt he'll head for a bar since he's off for the rest of the night. Tell him where I left the invitation and he'll find it for you.''

If he was gone long enough for her to get on board and find Joel Faber...

"Ma'am, I can't leave my post."

"Oh, stuff and nonsense!" she half laughed, throwing an arch look at the second guard. "What do you think I'm going to do? Rape your boss?"

She won an appreciative chuckle, and with her adrenaline running at an all-time high she seized the advantage, pressing on good-humoredly. "Come on, you guys! There are two of you. It's not wholesale desertion of duty if only one does me a favour."

Then in a flash of pure inspiration, she lifted her left hand and wriggled her fingers, drawing attention to the beautiful pearl ring that Armand had given her one heady night in Noumea. "Mr Faber did give me a very special invitation," she said suggestively. "And I'm already running late. I'll be with him if you still want to check me out when you come back."

And if that didn't nail it, nothing would, Tiffany decided. She stepped past them, arrogantly assuming that any argument was at an end. She half expected a restraining hand to fall on her shoulder. Her whole body was tensed to reject it, her mind feverishly preparing an outraged response.

\*    \*    \*

JOEL WATCHED the security men as they looked at each other with uncertainty, but neither moved to stop the woman. She had outfoxed and outfaced them with style, and he was vastly amused by the performance. He gave it a slow hand-clap, startling her into looking up at him. Their eyes locked, and he smiled at the shock of recognition on her face. For a moment he savoured the power he had to deny her, but he admired the gutsy deception she had just carried off, and he was intrigued enough to want to find out more about her.

"I've been waiting for you," he said, and in a way that was true. Something unpredictable... different. So what if she was a girl on the make, going after the main chance! It was a fine bit of calculation with all the wealthy men on his guest list tonight. Such a clever operator deserved a reward for effort even though he couldn't allow her to fool his guests.

There was a flicker of confusion on her face before understanding dawned. Her mouth curled in ironic appreciation of his complicity. He had caught her red-handed, so to speak—they both knew it—but he was letting her get away with it.

"Sorry! I was held up," she lilted up at him, keeping the act going as though she hadn't missed a pace. Gutsy and very quick on the uptake. "Don't move. I'll be with you in a minute," she added with a fervour that surprised him. No sense of guilt whatsoever.

"I'll be most aggrieved if you're not," he replied, a mocking threat in his drawl.

She laughed, whether from relief or jubilation he couldn't quite tell. But it didn't matter. He liked the sound of her laughter. It was unaffected, a ripple of natural delight. Joel suddenly realised the flat empty feeling was gone. In its place was a delicious sense of anticipation.

He hoped that further acquaintance with her wouldn't prove a disappointment. He noticed she had a very sexy bottom as she walked jauntily along the boardwalk to the ramp that led on to the yacht. A surprise package in more ways than one, he thought, and laughed softly to himself. He had expected a woman to make some move on him—it invariably happened—but not one with quite so much enterprise. The encounter should be interesting if nothing else.

# CHAPTER THREE

TIFFANY COULD HARDLY believe her luck. She certainly hadn't anticipated Joel Faber actually watching her act and playing along with it. Why had he done it? she wondered. Was he amused by her bold effrontery, indulging it on a whim of the moment? Or did he relish giving her a personal ticking off before turning her away? Not that it mattered. She had the chance she had planned for. That was the important thing.

As she stepped on to the deck of *Liberty* she glanced back down the gangplank. Neither of the security guards had moved to go to the hotel. The issue of the invitation had been summarily dropped. After Joel Faber's suggestive greeting, the men weren't about to question her right to be here.

Tiffany's heart skipped a beat as she thought about that suggestiveness. Apart from his position of wealth and power, and the fact that he had remained conspicuously single among much-married millionaires, she didn't know what kind of man Joel Faber was. But if he had any funny ideas about her, she would soon set him straight. And surely once she told him why she had come, their meeting would be put on to a totally proper footing.

Her mind was too occupied by the imminent confrontation to register the curious glances thrown her way as she threaded through the crowd of guests, moving purposefully towards the rear deck. Besides, she wasn't particularly interested in celebrities and socialites. They were nothing new to her. She had seen and met plenty of them in her varied career. She had come to see only one person tonight and he was waiting for her.

Joel Faber was taking two glasses of champagne from a waiter's tray when she spotted him, still against the railing from where he had called down to her. He hadn't moved. She skirted the last group of people and then there was no one between them ... only a few feet of deck and a queer sense of precognition—as if this man had always been waiting somewhere along the track of her life—and now ... now he was here, directly in front of her.

Maybe the feeling was caused by her obsession about reaching him, Tiffany reasoned. For months he had been on her mind. Perhaps it was simply an emotional reaction to having finally attained this personal meeting. And yet...despite having seen a recent photograph of him she wasn't at all prepared for the weird impact he made on her now.

For one thing, she hadn't expected him to be so tall—at least six feet—and the impressive breadth of chest and shoulders suggested a muscular solidity. Yet his face had a lean and hungry look—all sharp angles and hollow cheeks as if he never had enough food. His hair was very dark, almost black, its straight wiry thickness tamed by a stylish cut. But he wasn't tamed. The photograph had made him look like a suave sophisticate, but Tiffany had only to look into those black fathomless eyes to sense the savage in him. Wealth and success and easy living hadn't softened him one bit. He was hard, this man, with the hardness of a survivor who had battled against extreme odds and emerged the winner. Yet there was no joy in him, only a patient vigilance.

"I'm not going to bite...yet," he drawled, his mouth quirking into a smile that was startlingly sensual.

He held out one of the champagne glasses to her, inviting her to step closer, to come all the way to him. His eyes mocked any reluctance on her part, and Tiffany couldn't explain to herself why she suddenly wanted to hang back, to keep her distance.

He exuded a male sexuality that made her intensely aware of being a woman. She had felt that kind of chemistry before...with Armand. It was nothing new. And she was sure it wasn't what made her feel so oddly vulnerable. She was not afraid of sex and she was experienced enough not to let any situation overwhelm her. She studied his face a moment longer, exerting every instinct to discern what was disturbing her, but the idea—when it came—was even more disturbing.

She tried to shake it off but somehow it couldn't be dislodged. Whether it was the words he had used, or the fine gauntness of his cheekbones, or the magnetic depths of those dark eyes, she didn't know, but her mind and heart were caught by the concept of hunger: a deep abiding hunger that had never been answered and never expected to be. And she had the awful feeling she was the next item on his menu, to be chewed up and swallowed when she failed to satisfy him.

"Let me warn you now that if you bite I invariably bite back," Tiffany said impulsively, forgetting that she was supposed to be employing the art of diplomacy, or that she was in no position to challenge him in any way. She should be meek, submissive, imploring. Somehow the man himself made that quite impossible. The need to assert herself as someone over whom he had no control was too compelling.

His soft laugh raised prickles all over her skin. More to deny his effect on her than to satisfy any thirst she had, Tiffany stepped forward and took the offered glass of champagne. "Thank you," she said, and much to her mortification the words came out huskily. Her throat was dry and tight. She lifted the glass to him in a mock toast, then gratefully sipped the cold bubbly wine.

"Kingfisher-blue," he murmured. His face seemed to tighten for a moment, then relaxed into a sardonic little smile. "It's a long time since I've seen eyes of that colour. It's very...distinctive.''

"I can take no credit for the colour," Tiffany returned dryly, refusing to be flattered by his compliment. "It's due to a recessive gene. Purely an accident of birth."

He was amused by the disclaimer. "Shall we say you were blessed?"

She shrugged. "If it pleases you."

"Surely it pleases you," he mocked. "How many men have you seduced with those eyes?"

"None," she said flatly, quite certain that she was not given to seduction and that she herself was unseduceable. Joel Faber was simply playing with her as though she were a new toy that might give him diversion for a while, so just for good measure she added, "And I have absolutely no intention of using them to seduce you."

Again that soft laugh. His lips made an extremely sensual teasing movement as he replied, "I'm not averse to you trying. A mysterious lady of the night...what could be more provocative?"

Tiffany determinedly quelled the flutters in her stomach. However physically attractive she found him, however challenging he was in character, she was not here to be played with. ''Is that why you let me gate-crash your party?'' she asked. She drew herself up a little more stiffly. ''Is that what you really thought? Here is a little temptation, a little pleasure....''

''Perhaps,'' he replied enigmatically. ''You wanted to be with me. Now you are. I am breathlessly waiting for your next move.''

The incongruity of his being breathless about anything made Tiffany laugh. Everything about him shouted this was a man in control of his own destiny, and there was nothing in the world that could surprise him. Watch...wait...test...pounce...that was how he operated. Tiffany could feel it in her bones.

''I'm sorry to disappoint you,'' she said, her voice still bubbling with laughter, ''but I have no designs on your body.''

''What a pity!'' His eyes flirted with hers, an appealing mixture of amusement and speculation. ''You mean I shall have to exert myself to change your mind?''

She grinned. ''Do you ever? Exert yourself over a woman?''

"Not often," he admitted unashamedly. "But I am always prepared to find an exception."

"Which is probably a measure of your boredom," Tiffany mocked. "Which entirely suits my purpose," she added while she sternly reminded herself that she was not here for flirtation, however tempting that might be. "I'm glad you're bored. It means I have a chance of interesting you in a new project. And that's what I do have on my mind."

"Ah..." he drawled, his mouth curling with cynicism. "Well, at least it's refreshing to get to the bottom line first. It saves so much pretending—" his half-shuttered eyes made a leisurely appraisal of her more obvious curves "—although, with you, I might have enjoyed pretending for a while."

A surge of heat scorched up Tiffany's long neck. "I'm not in the game of trading sexual favours, Mr Faber," she said stiffly. "I couldn't think of anything more repulsive. I came to you for help. A straight unvarnished deal."

One eyebrow lifted in mocking challenge as his gaze met hers with hard derision. "Very prettily packaged to offer your deal. You've used your assets very convincingly."

"That was to pass scrutiny. To be a convincing guest," she retorted emphatically, her eyes defying any other interpretation he might make of her appearance. "You've made yourself a very unapproachable man, Mr Faber. Which created difficulties. You've caused me a great deal more trouble than I'm generally used to. I've been trying to get your ear for months now."

He shrugged, making no apology. "You and a thousand others who don't give a damn about me or anything else, except insofar as they can use me to do what they want. That's always the name of the game. The bottom line." He paused to lend a wicked emphasis to his next taunt. "So how much money do you want?"

Perhaps it was the note of scorn in his voice, the sense of having been judged and found unworthy, of being nothing in his eyes. It made Tiffany feel cheap, ugly, dismissed. Anger churned through her. What right did he have to dismiss her so contemptuously without so much as a hearing?

"I'm not here for a handout," she shot at him fiercely. "I can give you something in return—"

"What can you give me?" he asked with cynical amusement.

"A sense of purpose, a sense of belonging."

An old, old weariness dragged at his features and he spoke in a tired voice. "That's enough. Get to the point. I meet a lot of people who are full of righteous fervour for their causes, and I don't want a sermon. I'll take it for granted that you are another do-gooder since you claim to be uninterested in sharing my bed. Just save me the do-gooding. With repetition it becomes incredibly boring. I'm not in the mood for it tonight. Since the bottom line is invariably money, simply tell me how much you need and I'll consider it."

The hot blood drained from her face as her anger twisted into shame. She *had* come to use him. She was as selfish in her need as anybody else. Blind. Not considering deeply enough that he had needs, too, needs never answered if her intuition wasn't playing her false. Just because he hid them behind a hard cynical shell didn't make them any less real.

She wanted to tell him she wanted nothing from him, but it wasn't true. And she couldn't back down now. Carol's and Alan's hopes for the future were dependent on a successful outcome to this meeting. Or some other meeting with someone else if she failed to interest Joel Faber.

"I'm sorry you feel that way," she said with quiet sincerity. "I wish I didn't have to ask you for help. It isn't much fun being on the asking end, either. But you're the one person who can achieve what is needed. It's not money so much as your backing and expertise that is required. And there truly is a return in it for you."

"What return?" The words were laced with intense scepticism.

"Satisfaction more than anything else," Tiffany said slowly, aware that financial return was probably not high on his list of priorities. If this yacht was anything to go by, Joel Faber had undoubtedly made more money than he knew what to do with.

There was a flicker of reluctant interest in his eyes. "Don't stop now. I'm intrigued to know what you imagine will satisfy me."

"You made Leisure Island happen. You were the impetus, the driving force behind it. Surely that's given you some satisfaction," Tiffany posed, feeling her way cautiously.

"Some," he conceded, his mouth quirking in appreciation of her argument.

"Wouldn't it give you a greater degree of satisfaction to make something happen for a place that has more claim on you than a fortuitous piece of land? To be the driving force—"

His lips tightened into a thin line and hard rejection flashed from his eyes. "No place has any claim on me," he stated coldly. "I buy. I sell. I have no attachments to anyone or anything. I belong nowhere. I think that conclusively dismisses your arguments. So, my lady of the night, what other compelling attraction do you have up your sleeve? Make your next move."

The chilling loneliness of his existence appalled Tiffany. To have no one, nowhere he called home.... She shuddered at the thought of having such a dreadful void in one's life. Having always had ready access to a huge family and a host of friends, she could hardly comprehend it. Joel Faber's success had cer-

tainly cost him dear if this was the result of
it.

"I know it's been twenty years, but doesn't
Haven Bay have some call on you?" she
asked, unable to believe it meant nothing at
all to him. There had to have been some happy
years in his childhood that brought back fond
memories.

He stared at her from a stillness that
screamed of tension. It wound around
Tiffany, constricting her breath, freezing her
mind, making her pulse skitter in frantic
protest at what she had unwittingly triggered
in him. Something dreadful had suddenly
materialised unseen, totally obscure to her,
but throbbing with a reality that was almost
tangible.

"Those eyes..." The words were a mere
wisp of breath escaping from some lost tortured world. Then in a harsh strident tone,
"Who did this? Who sent you?"

"No one. It was my idea."

"Who are your parents? Your relatives?"

Tiffany was completely bewildered. But
since she had no blood relatives at all—to her
knowledge—her answer was straightforward.
"I haven't any," she said firmly, needing to

get some grasp on the situation. "None in the absolute literal meaning of the word. Although in another sense, I'm from a very large family. The very best."

"Tell me your name," Joel Faber barked.

"Tiffany James," she answered automatically.

"James..." He echoed it as if turning it over in his mind, testing it for some relevant connection.

The thought came to her that Garret should have told her, warned her, although what the old fisherman had kept to himself was totally indistinct. Then, to Tiffany's further confusion, Joel Faber turned and casually tipped the contents of his champagne glass into the sea. Somehow it was like a very deliberate statement that this party was over as far as he was concerned. When he turned back to her it was with a markedly withdrawn air. All the sexual magnetism he had emanated earlier was completely switched off, and the taut reserve in his eyes kept her firmly at a distance.

"I think we will continue this conversation in my stateroom," he said, more in the nature of a command than a suggestion. His mouth curled. "Let's keep it private. You can spell out what's on your mind without any fear of distraction or interruption, Tiffany James. But be aware of one thing. I'll get to the bottom of this...conspiracy. I'll also get to the bottom of you.''

He lifted his hand and drew a savage line down her cheek with his index finger. ''Be aware that you are playing with forces that are almost...irresistible. If they go out of control, you have no one to blame but yourself.''

His decision should have pleased her. He was giving her the opportunity she wanted. Yet his words were so ominous, so threatening, that she felt extremely uneasy about the whole situation. Certainly whatever initial attraction she might have had for him had been wiped out in the past few moments, so she had no concern over any sexual design in this move. But the idea of being completely alone with him, in his present inscrutable mood, was totally disquieting.

He didn't wait for her assent anyway. He took charge, drawing her after him as he weaved through the crowd of people, signalling to a waiter who collected their glasses from them, briefly acknowledging comments thrown at him, effectively turning aside any attempt to halt their progress.

Tiffany followed him in silent accord, firmly telling herself she had nothing to fear. She was not part of any conspiracy and her life was a completely open book. As far as she was concerned, there was nothing to get to the bottom of, although she was intensely curious as to why Joel Faber thought there was. What did Haven Bay mean to him?

From his reaction so far, Tiffany was acutely aware that there was a lot she didn't know, and once again she privately railed against Garret McKeogh for leaving her in ignorance. Although it was possible that the old fisherman didn't know, either, or he had thought it wiser not to cloud her approach to Joel Faber with any issue from the past.

Nevertheless, Tiffany couldn't help wondering what the colour of her eyes had to do with anything. And what were the irresistible forces that could go out of control? The unrelenting strength of the hand that held hers captured was certainly one of them.

There was no reason at all for the distracting attraction she felt toward this powerful stranger. However, it was patently obvious that, with Joel Faber's outlook on life, it could lead nowhere good. Therefore it had to be blocked or ignored. She had come to him for one purpose only and she had to keep her mind set firmly on her mission. That was the important thing.

# CHAPTER FOUR

Joel Faber opened the door to his stateroom and waved Tiffany inside. She stepped past him, extremely aware of something distinctly predatory emanating from him. Her eyes flicked nervously around the luxurious stateroom: the lustre of the panelled woodwork, the paintings on the walls, the expensive furniture, the thick plushness of the carpet, the king-size bed....

The click of the door shutting behind her made Tiffany's heart kick an extra beat. She jerked around, instinctively facing danger. Joel Faber leaned back against the closed door, pointedly blocking any retreat. Not that Tiffany wanted to retreat. She was determined to put her project to him, no matter what! But somehow the threat he had made up on the deck seemed far more real in the intimate privacy of his room.

His mouth curled but there was no smile in the glittering dark eyes. They mocked her tension. "Not feeling so brave now, Miss James?" he drawled.

"As brave as I need to be, Mr Faber," she insisted, defiantly holding his gaze. "I have nothing to hide."

"Meaning I have?" he shot at her.

"Have you?" she asked.

He gave a soft little laugh that sent prickles down her spine. "My dear Miss James, what secrets I have are very much my own. And they shall stay my own."

He pushed away from the door and walked over to a cupboard on the far side of the bed. He opened a box of cigars, picked out one, trimmed it with a savage little movement, then lit it. His head tilted back slightly as he dragged in the fragrant smoke. Then he swung around slowly, a gleam of hard challenge in his eyes. He lifted the cigar in casual enquiry. "Does this worry you?"

It was as if he were defying her to criticise his smoking habits, wanting to pounce on her for any reason at all. And tear her apart. "No," she replied simply, denying him that satisfaction. She didn't understand what was going on in his mind, but the tension emanating from him made her feel very uncomfortable.

He waved toward the two armchairs grouped close to where she still stood. "Sit down. Tell me about yourself. I shall be fascinated to hear the remarkable chain of events that has led you to my door...so to speak."

The words tripped out without any real sincerity, a glib pretence of interest, and she hesitated, pricklingly aware that this controlled carelessness belied his true feelings. She preferred to be on her feet with him. But that was a personal feeling, and Tiffany sternly reminded herself that to waste all her effort in reaching him by getting sidetracked on personal issues was not answering the need that had brought her here. She had no meeting place with Joel Faber...apart from business.

She moved decisively, laying down her jacket and handbag on one chair before settling on the other. She felt him watching her, the sensation so sharp that it made her absurdly conscious of her body. She sat down and crossed her legs, hoping to minimise the discomfort of jangling nerves.

Having recollected her sense of purpose, Tiffany steeled herself to look up at him as calmly and coolly as she could. He was viewing her through the narrowed slits of hooded eyes and she could not discern what he was thinking. His face was totally expressionless.

"The humpback whales have come back to Haven Bay," she said, wanting to capture his interest from the outset. And hold it, as best she could. She saw the flicker of surprise in his eyes and plunged on, hoping he would give her a fair hearing.

"You must remember them. The old-timers say the whales always used to come to Haven Bay when you were a boy. But then they were near extinction, down to the last few hundred, and the sightings got fewer and fewer...."

He frowned, clearly not liking what she was saying, but he didn't interrupt her.

"They started returning a few years ago, and more are coming all the time," she pressed on eagerly. "Perhaps it's because the bay is sheltered from the southerly busters. There are a lot of theories. The water is warm and placid. Whatever it is, they keep coming. Alan counted up to a thousand last year. And people are really aware of whales now, what fantastic creatures they are."

She drew a quick breath. "We could get a lot of tourists coming to see them. If we provided all the right amenities and publicised in the right places, I'm sure we could draw them. Make a thriving industry of it. It's simply a matter of expertise—"

"You don't know what you're talking about," he cut in decisively. "You have no idea what it takes to—"

"On the contrary, I have every idea of what it takes to attract tourists," she asserted vehemently.

One eyebrow lifted in mocking scepticism. "What background do you have in the business?"

"For most of the past three years I've been on the Club Méditerranée staff in Noumea. Before that I worked travel tours in New Zealand and did resort publicity for Fiji. I've also done adventure tours in the Himalayas and Tibet, and gone down the Silk Road of China. I doubt there's anything you can tell me about what tourists want, Mr Faber."

"A very eventful life," he commented in an acid drawl. "So what have you graduated to now?" He took a puff of his cigar. "What do you want me for?" The smoke drifted from his lips, forming a distorting veil over stonelike features.

Tiffany swallowed the acid in his words. This was the moment when she had to spell it out. The carrot first, she thought, and then the meat. She kept her own tone light and businesslike. ''Initially I want your backing for a television documentary on the whales at Haven Bay.''

''Then I must say no! You're talking about an investment of some hundreds of thousands of dollars—''

''It won't be that much,'' Tiffany quickly assured him. ''Not with your help! I can get it done for nothing! Practically nothing anyway.''

''Rubbish!''

''I'm going to use my family.''

His eyes narrowed. ''You'd better explain this family of yours,'' he demanded tersely.

''It's very large. There are fourteen of us. We all had the same foster parents and we all help one another. I've already done quite a few television videos for tourism advertising. I know how it's done. But more importantly, I worked in television before the travel business, and one of my brothers is a top TV executive. He can get the cameraman. We can make the documentary for the cost of the film. You'll get value out of it by showing it on Q2RV. You'll be the first in on it, and then you can sell it to other networks. You can make money out of this. If you want to.''

He frowned at her, whether in disbelief or disapproval she wasn't sure. ''What's in it for you?''

They had come to the crunch and she had to get him onside. The documentary wasn't so important. Her brother could handle that without any backing from Joel Faber, if the worst came to the worst. But for what they really needed, a resort development, there was no one better than this man. Tiffany took a deep breath and plunged ahead.

''Haven Bay is dying. Like so many fishing villages it's become an anachronism. And I want to save it. The fishing industry barely sustains the township now. There aren't any jobs for the young people. The future is hopeless unless we can drag it by the scruff of the neck into the twenty-first century. That means another industry. And it's there. Tourism, waiting to be tapped. I know it is. But we need help.''

"Who is we?" He bit out the words as though they were distasteful to him.

"I guess you could say the whole community. And since Haven Bay was your old hometown, we thought...I thought..." she amended quickly, troubled by the bitter flash of scorn in his eyes. "It's all been my idea, really. And I know it will work. All it needs is the right promotion and the right amenities for—"

"Not from me," he cut in savagely. "I will not lift one finger to do one damned thing for the community of Haven Bay. I hate the place. I hate what it did to me, and what it did to others. As far as I'm concerned, all that was good in it died twenty years ago. For me, it *is* dead. And I have no desire whatsoever to resurrect it!"

He punched out the last words with passion, and they fell like angry blows on Tiffany's head, dazing her. She stared at him, barely able to believe what she had heard. He stood like a patriarch of old, stonelike in his judgement, his lips thinned white in grim decision, his eyes like burning black holes of hell and damnation.

Although his gaze was directed at her, she felt he did not see her at all, and when he spoke again it was in a bare whisper, words dragged from his soul and given voice for his own satisfaction. "I'll be glad to see it die. Then everything will have found its final place." He turned and stubbed his cigar into an ashtray, grinding it out as if he'd like to grind out the whole human race.

*Old Garret knew,* she thought. He had known how Joel Faber would react. Yet he had encouraged her to go on with her idea, until virtually the last minute. Why? Had the two men meant something to each other once? Was there some terrible connection between them that still had the power to distort their lives?

"Do you remember Garret McKeogh?" she blurted out. "Does he mean anything to you?"

His back stiffened. Slowly, ever so slowly, he swung around, his face a pale tight mask from which his dark eyes bored into her like laser beams. "Is he at the bottom of this?" he demanded.

"No. I told you, it's my idea. But he warned me I was unlikely to find you co-operative."

His mouth curled in ironic acknowledgment. "You would have saved yourself a lot of time and effort had you listened to him."

"Why? It's been twenty years!" she cried heatedly, driven to question his edict by an overwhelming sense of wasteful futility. "Even if you weren't happy there, and your grandfather died in the storm, how can you hold such a grudge against a place?"

"That is none of your business, Miss James, and I don't care to have anyone prying into my life," he stated icily. "Nor would I recommend it," he added, the implied threat clearly not an idle one.

She flushed. "I'm not prying. All I'm saying is that whatever you have against Haven Bay was a generation ago. None of the young people there now did anything against you." Her eyes filled with eloquent appeal. "Won't you help them?"

When he didn't answer, she pleaded their cause more passionately. "They shouldn't be blamed. Whatever the sins of the fathers, you have no reason to visit them on their sons. That's neither fair nor just!"

"Fair! Just!" he snorted contemptuously. "If you're looking for fairness or justice in this world, you're on a futile quest!"

It was hopeless. He wasn't going to budge from his position, no matter what she said. And maybe he had reason for his stance, although she did not understand it. To her it was too extreme, too unforgiving, too relentless. But she couldn't see anything she could do about it. With a deep sigh of disappointment she pushed herself out of her chair.

"There's nothing I can say that will change your mind?" she asked, still reluctant to give up even with defeat staring her in the face.

"Nothing!" he affirmed harshly.

Tiffany didn't know what moved her feet towards him: a sense of guilt for stirring up a dormant pain, a need to appease it in some way, a desire to make some amends for having blindly intruded on something so deeply etched on his psyche that not even twenty years had blunted the memory.

His face was closed and shuttered to her, his body so tense that even his hands were tightly clenched at his sides as she came to a halt in front of him. She sensed an intensely wary watchfulness in the gleaming slits of his hooded eyes. *The survivor,* she thought, *but at what cost?*

She reached up and softly stroked his cheek, instinctively using the gentling touch she would have used on any wounded creature. "Why?" she asked, trying to probe the inner mysteries of his soul. "You could have been a decent man. What could have made you like this?"

He looked as if he had been hit by a bolt of lightning. Totally transfixed. Then a storm of violent emotion warred across his face and his hand came up to close vicelike around her wrist, dragging her arm back, forcibly preventing any further touch from her.

"What are you?" he rasped. "Some kind of nemesis sent to haunt me?"

She shook her head, more in compassion than denial. "You're so alone. I wish I could find something to do for you."

All colour drained from his face. "Damn those eyes! Do you know what you're doing to me?"

Before she could think what he meant, or make any reply, his arm had swept her body against his and the hand that had held her wrist was raking through her hair, his fingers entangling themselves in the long silky tresses, tilting her head back. Then his mouth was on hers, seeking, searching, wanting, imparting a need so great that Tiffany could not help responding. She didn't even consider that in opening her mouth to the insistence of his she was inadvertently opening the gates to the insatiable hunger she had sensed in him in those first moments of meeting.

He kissed her with such ravaging passion that Tiffany was dizzied by a whirlwind of sensation. She clung to him in sheer mindless necessity, too weakened by his need to tear herself away. She felt as though he were drawing all he could from her, and the more he drew the more he wanted. She felt invaded by him, enveloped by him, and the compelling power of the man stirred turbulent feelings she had never felt before. She was limp and shaken to the depths of her being when he finally lifted his mouth away from hers, and then he was kissing her eyelids, her temples, sweeping her fringe aside with his lips, breathing passionate warmth through her hair as he tasted its clean silky texture.

"I must have all of you," he murmured, his fingertips grazing softly down her throat, down the edge of the deep neckline of her silk vest.

"No." She could barely find the strength of mind to speak, and her voice was a hoarse croak.

His lips teased her ear. "You want me," he whispered. "I'll make it good for you."

"No." She dragged in a deep breath and forced herself to push a little distance between them. "You only want to take, not give."

"I'll give you every pleasure I can think of," he promised huskily.

Yes, she thought, he probably would be a generous lover, but afterward she would be just another body that had given him some brief satisfaction. And Tiffany didn't want a relationship that would only be sexual. Not with him. Not with anyone. She needed more.

Joel Faber's world was far removed from hers. And Armand's ring on her finger was the eternal reminder that rich men only took nonentities like her as mistresses, not wives. Stupid to ever make that mistake again. This was the only meeting place she had with Joel

Faber, now that their business was over, and she *didn't* want it.

She lifted her hands to his face and pulled it back from hers so that she could look into his eyes. Black fathomless eyes that would be so easy to lose herself in. But there was no future in that.

"I can't reach you, can I? You only want forgetfulness. That's what you'd use me for," she said, intuitively knowing it was true. "And I'm not good at walking away afterward."

"Perhaps I wouldn't want you to," he answered, his voice still furred with need. "Stay with me. Try it."

"Joel . . . I've been down that road. It's the loneliest road in the world, and there's only hurt at the end of it. *La petite mort* they call it, the little death. And it's even more so in an emotional sense when there's no binding love. Isn't that so?"

A shadow of his earlier torment tightened his face. "Why do you talk to me like this?"

Concern threaded her soft reply. "Hasn't anyone? Ever?"

"Don't! It's too late!" he said harshly.

"No No, it's not, Joel. It's never too late to learn what loving is about."

Cynicism thinned his mouth. "You're working your way back to your project, aren't you?"

"I'm sorry you think that," she said sadly, knowing that she'd lost him. Even this meeting ground was too tenuous to sustain, and impossible to recapture now with his hard cynical shell falling back into place. "It's time for me to go."

He did not try to hold her as she turned out of his embrace. Nor did he make any move after her as she walked back across the room, disappointment dragging at every step. She picked up her handbag and jacket, pulled together her pride and dignity and swung around to face him again. He was watching her with a darkly brooding look. She stretched her lips into a polite smile.

"Thank you for your time. I hope I haven't completely spoilt your party for you."

"Like the feelings between us, Haven Bay won't work, Tiffany!" he said tensely.

Somehow she pitched her own voice to light enquiry. "Why?"

"I know that place in intimate detail. The logistics simply aren't favourable and the scale is all wrong. Even with the whales, take my word for it, you'll only have a tourist sideline, day-trippers, not enough to build an industry that could revitalise a town."

Her face set in stubbornness. "Other places have less, and they've made it. Noosa is an example. It doesn't even have much of a beach. Boats can't go into it—"

"What of the risk that the whales might go away again?" he slipped in with chilling pointedness.

Tiffany refused to let him undermine her argument. "Noosa doesn't have whales. It works."

He waved a dismissive hand. "It's been built up over a large number of years."

"We'll build up Haven Bay," she replied with determination, her disappointment turning to anger at his continued opposition, especially after she had tried her best to understand him. "The more popular we make it, the more money coming in, the more business it will attract," she asserted. "The trawlers can be used to take people out for a close view of the whales. We can get tearooms going. Guest house accommodation. What we need right now is a publicity drive, and television tells it better than anything else.''

''You said you wanted my expertise.'' Impatience sharpened his voice. ''You're getting it. I'm telling you the odds are against you. Give it up. The project won't work!''

''That judgement wouldn't be warped by prejudice, would it?'' Tiffany retorted fiercely. ''If you had wanted to help us...''

''You won't get any big developer interested!'' he insisted vehemently. Then with a forced return to cynicism, ''Unless you can prove there's money to be made.''

Her eyes flashed defiant determination. ''Then I'll prove it. And you'll be the loser, Joel Faber, because Haven Bay will attract big business.''

He sighed. Heavily. Then grimaced for good measure. ''Some things, Tiffany James, sound like fine ideas at the time. When you try to implement them in a practical, pragmatic world they simply don't work. And since you mentioned Q2RV, I'll cite that as an example. It seemed like a fine idea when I bought it. Three general managers later, I'm not so sure. Not one of them has been able to get the ratings up. Obviously it can be done—''

''It wouldn't be hard!'' Tiffany sliced in with almost contemptuous disregard for the problem.

''I beg your pardon?'' He frowned at her.

''It wouldn't be hard,'' she repeated. ''It's pretty obvious to the general viewer what's wrong with it.''

''Well, it's not to anyone else in the industry,'' he retorted pointedly.

''If I couldn't do a better job of it, I'd cut my throat,'' she declared, completely unabashed.

His mouth twitched in sardonic amusement. ''Unfortunately, the managers I employed weren't so helpful. I had to fire each and every one of them.''

Tiffany stared at that smile. Was he relaxing his opposition? Had she reached something inside him? If she could hook his interest, all was not yet lost. More in hope than with any conviction, she asked, ''If I suggested to you ways to get your ratings up, would you back the documentary I want to make on Haven Bay? And give it prime airtime? I promise you it would be good viewing.''

That would be a start, Tiffany thought. After that he might be prepared to give Haven Bay the time and the investment it required.

He eyed her speculatively for what seemed a very long time before he shook his head. Tiffany, who had been holding her breath, hoping against hope, couldn't stop herself from fighting his decision. She desperately wanted him to change his mind, not only for Haven Bay, but for the opportunity to share more time with him, to get to know more about him.

''I could do it,'' she pleaded. ''The ratings, I mean. One of my brothers has just achieved that for a Sydney television channel. You should know his name...Zachary Lee James. Everybody's after his expertise.''

''And you could get him for me?'' Joel Faber asked, an interested gleam leaping into his eyes.

''No. Zachary Lee is settled in Sydney. But I can get his advice. We always help one another in our family.''

''So you said,'' he murmured.

He walked across the room to her in a slow purposeful way that had Tiffany holding her breath again. She was swept by an extreme physical awareness of the man as he came to a halt a bare half pace away. The dark eyes held hers with urgent intensity.

''Forget Haven Bay, Tiffany. If developing the tourist industry is what you're about, come and work with me. I can use your talents in my organisation.''

The desire to keep her in his life throbbed behind every word, and if the circumstances had been other than they were Tiffany knew she would have grasped his offer with grateful eagerness, however foolhardy that might be in a personal sense. As it was, he was asking the impossible.

''I wish it could have been different,'' she said, her voice husky with painful regret. ''But I've got to make Haven Bay work. It's for my sister and her son. They need it. I can't let them down.''

She saw the retreat in his eyes, the rejection, and suddenly Tiffany couldn't take any more. She felt like crying, and she hadn't cried since Armand. Tears were lonely things. She wouldn't let it happen.

"Thank you for the offer, Joel. Maybe...one day. I must go now," she said briskly, then headed straight for the door, not waiting for any reply.

Somehow he got there before her, opening it for her to pass through. "I'll see you out," he murmured.

She didn't argue. She couldn't speak. There was an awful lump in her throat. She was extremely sensitive to Joel's closeness as he followed her along the gangway to the door at the end of it. This led to the huge saloon where the main body of the party was undoubtedly still raging. Once through there, the parting of the ways would be effected. She summoned up a brave smile as he leaned past her to open the door.

With her whole mind and body tightly concentrated on her departure from Joel Faber's life, Tiffany was totally unprepared for the sudden furore that broke out around her when she stepped into the saloon. An explosion of light dazzled her eyes. She threw up her arm to ward it off and half stumbled backward. The next instant she was pulled in against Joel's body, his arm around her waist in a tight protective hold.

"Well, Joel, after all this time, we've finally got you cold!" a woman's voice drawled exultantly. "You might as well give in gracefully and make the announcement."

# CHAPTER FIVE

NORMALLY TIFFANY would have handled any spotlight with ease. She was used to addressing people, whether tour groups or hotel parties or millions of imaginary viewers. She was rarely caught at a disadvantage. But this time she was in a weakened condition, both emotionally and physically, and she could not disguise the fact. She was completely at a loss even to know what was happening. All she could think of was how good it felt to lean against the strength of Joel Faber as he took charge of the situation.

"Whatever mistaken notion you have, Nerida——" he began curtly, then broke off to direct a blast at the photographers who were still popping off flashlights. "Keep that up and you'll be thrown off the yacht in no time flat," he stated grimly.

"Now, now, Joel," the woman chided. "There had to be an answer to your antisocial behaviour over the last three months, and now we've got it. The very fact that you hid it from everyone stresses its importance to you. So typical. But your secret affair is well and truly blown. A picture of you and your fiancée is big news, and you can't begrudge me the scoop." She looked pointedly at Tiffany. "So let's start with the lady's name."

Fiancée! The word rattled around Tiffany's skull until her dazed mind splintered with the shock of it. The realisation that she was being linked to Joel Faber in such intimate terms forced an instant denial off her tongue.

"There is no romantic involvement whatsoever between Mr Faber and myself!" she snapped. "And never will be." She was appalled that he should be subjected to such gossip mongering on her account. However unwitting it had been, she had already given him more than enough mental torment tonight.

The woman confronting them was incredibly self-assured. Somewhere in her late forties, Tiffany judged, but a very polished sophisticate; her short blonde hair artfully styled to flatter her narrow face, her slim figure poured into a peach satin gown, her bright blue eyes full of cynical worldliness. She smiled condescendingly at Tiffany.

"The 'just-good-friends' comment is too late. I'm afraid you've given the game away."

"The game, if you want to call it that, was strictly business," Tiffany declared heatedly. "To imply anything else is ridiculous!"

"I am surprised at you, Nerida," Joel sliced in a smooth sardonic drawl. "You don't usually get your wires crossed. Be kind enough to humour me. What induced you to leap to such an unwarranted conclusion? Simply the fact that I've been out of the social limelight these past three months?"

She laughed at him, her confidence not the slightest bit shaken. And Tiffany noticed that many of the onlookers wore knowing grins. It was now impossible for her to slip away unnoticed.

"It won't do you any good to be coy, Joel," the woman stated with all the satisfaction of a piranha that had caught its prey and was starting to tear it to shreds. "Your restlessness and uninterest was noted earlier on, as was your withdrawal from the party just before the lady arrived. Her remarks to the security guard, your response, your haste and single-mindedness in whisking her away for a very private tête-à-tête. Naturally it made us all curious. And on questioning the security guards, and so on, the conclusion seems inescapable—'' she paused, her eyes gleaming with triumph ''—one might almost say undeniable. The lady is wearing a particularly interesting ring on the third finger of her left hand.''

Tiffany barely stifled a groan at her reckless indiscretion on the jetty. And it was pure eccentricity of her to have kept Armand's ring on that finger. She had expected an engagement ring from him. She wore it there as an act of bitter irony after the truth of their relationship had finally become clear to her, and as an eternal reminder of the fickleness of men. But now she *had* to explain it away!

''This is totally ridiculous!'' She had to make the attempt, however thin it sounded. ''Anyone can see it's only a dress ring.'' She held up the offending ring, only to have the gesture greeted by knowing smiles of disbelief. And the fact was, the pearl was an exceptional one, and the diamonds surrounding it could hardly be called chips.

She threw an anguished look of apology up at Joel. ''I'll never know how to make this up to you. I certainly never meant to make this nuisance of myself.''

His hand dug into her waist. His eyes glittered briefly into hers, a hard hot savagery almost instantly curtained by a cold bleakness. He lifted his gaze to meet the swift darting glances of the reporter's knowingness. "You won't let go, will you, Nerida?" he said wearily. "You'll chase this thing to the bitter end.''

"Right to the bitter end," she agreed. "Weeks, months won't mean a thing to me. I've got you at last," she gloated. "I'll pursue it all the way down to the last step to the altar. I'll never let go.''

"Then in that case, you leave me no other option but to tell the whole truth, even though it is premature. If nothing else, it will save you the trouble of digging further, and in the wrong direction. Therefore, while it is not the time I would have chosen in normal circumstances, I will give you an announcement.''

An excited buzz ran around the room. The reporter's eyes lit with glee. Joel's fingers dug harder into Tiffany's waist. She anxiously wondered what he could say to get the reporter off their backs, but whatever it was she would support it. The kind of hounding Nerida threatened filled her with horror.

''Tonight I did not want to take any focus away from Leisure Island,'' Joel stated matter-of-factly. ''But since attention has been drawn to my meeting with Miss James, which was certainly meant to be private, I am pleased to announce that an agreement has now been reached between us. The low ratings at Q2RV are of considerable concern to me. We have been discussing the problem. Miss James has agreed to do a pilot for a special-interest show. Should that prove as popular as she expects, the management of Q2RV will be right behind her for any other initiatives she might propose. All the way to station manager. That's as much as I'm prepared to say at this time.''

Tiffany couldn't help throwing him a startled look. His words were so unbelievable! He could not have changed his mind about backing the documentary! It would mean he had just performed an about-face of incredible proportions. This might simply be a ploy to divert the society reporter from probing into their lives and having them followed wherever they might go.

Whatever the truth of it—and she could not allow herself to hope he really meant what he said—Tiffany's course was clear. She had a moral obligation to support his announcement. Joel Faber did not deserve to be pecked apart by this vulture of a woman. She resolved to follow him all the way in his deception. Then, as soon as this charade was played through, she would make her escape, and never see him again.

The fingers at her waist dug deeper. She looked up at him. His mouth smiled. The dark eyes held hers with burning command. She gave him a reassuring little nod.

"Miss James is quite certain she knows what the public wants," he said, then swept the smile to the surprised onlookers. "If she fails to draw viewers on the scale she anticipates, she has offered to commit a quite spectacular suicide. Which will at least be newsworthy, and should help the ratings."

The light toss-off line earned a few laughs, and Tiffany sensed a general easing of interest. Joel topped it off by turning back to the reporter and employing a mockingly indulgent tone. "So you can see, Nerida, what a mistake you have made. There is no love interest. As Miss James told you earlier, this is totally business.''

Titters broke out from the amused audience. Nerida threw him a look of hard-bitten scepticism. ''I'll reserve judgement, Joel. I don't believe you.''

Her eyes flicked over Tiffany in critical reappraisal before zeroing back to her prime target. ''Knowing you as I do, Joel,'' she drawled, ''I can see that Miss James is well qualified as a love interest. So, if you are to be believed, what qualifications does she have for the situation you've just outlined?''

''Initiative, enterprise and courage, Nerida,'' he answered coolly. ''Miss James has been working overseas in recent years, and is extremely convincing about the trends developing in popular taste. I think, perhaps, it's enough to say, for everyone in the know, that her brother is Zachary Lee James. It's a brave person who can discount his success in this particular area of expertise.''

The woman's eyes narrowed. Clearly she hated to be proved wrong. Particularly in public. Tiffany had the sharp impression of a hunter who had scented blood and was determined on stalking her quarry.

"You're not in the habit of placing women as decision makers in your organisation, Joel. You've never done it before in your whole career," she pointed out suspiciously. "This deal has all the hallmarks of a sexual *coup de main.*"

"New blood, Nerida. New blood. It's what Q2RV needs. And I'll promote anyone who's good enough, so don't lay a sexist tag on me. Now, if you'll excuse us, I had intended introducing Miss James to a few people less formally than this."

The arm around Tiffany's waist tightened and swept her firmly away from Nerida. He headed in among the guests, hailed someone, and Tiffany was promptly called upon to play the role Joel had assigned to her, or give the game away. She had no idea if she was acting out the truth or a lie, but she so passionately wanted it to be the truth that she had no trouble playing her part with conviction. In any event, it was the least she could do, since she had dragged this down upon Joel's head with her earlier act.

This time Tiffany was all discretion, aware that Nerida had her cynical blue eyes trained on them, ready to pounce on anything she could get her sharp claws into. This woman made her living from being a parasite on other people's lives.

The personal questions were easy enough for Tiffany to fend off. When asked about her previous experience, she gave an enigmatic smile and declared that she had a long string of successes in making things happen, and she preferred to let results speak for themselves rather than blow her own trumpet.

She refused to answer queries about the pilot show, insisting it remain a secret until they had stolen a march on everyone else. Privately she had decided Joel wouldn't want Haven Bay mentioned, couldn't want it under the circumstances. As time went on she became more and more convinced that this act was all a lie to avoid having his connection to Haven Bay turned into public titillation.

Joel's support of her performance was masterly; steering the conversation away from possible pitfalls, adding comments that lent an extra verisimilitude to everything she said, treating her with a respect that rubbed off on everyone they talked to: television personalities, owners of ad agencies, PR people, other Q2RV executives who were trying to show they were not overly concerned by Joel's announcement.

However treacherous it was, Tiffany revelled in the sense of togetherness imparted by the need for her and Joel to support each other. The occasional intimate flash of appreciation in his eyes stirred a faint hope that she might yet persuade him to change his mind about Haven Bay. It also gave her the craziest feeling that she belonged with him, and he with her. Sheer fantasy, she told herself, and knew it to be so when she brought the act to an end.

She had to be at the pier for Garret's return, and she felt they had done enough to put that Nerida woman off the track for tonight anyway. She touched Joel's arm and offered an apologetic smile to his sharply questioning eyes. "You'll have to excuse me. It's time for me to leave," she stated decisively.

"Of course," he agreed smoothly, but she saw a flash of bitter mockery in his eyes as he added, "It was good of you to stay so long." He extracted them both from their present company just as smoothly. "Please excuse us. I must see Miss James to her car."

Tiffany managed her enigmatic smile for the last time. Her face felt stiff. Her whole body felt stiff as Joel took her elbow to steer her out into the darkness of the night. She welcomed the end of the charade, yet despondently acknowledged it was also the end of the hope that had brought her here.

They reached the head of the gangplank to the jetty, and the cool air from the water hit Tiffany's bare arms and made her shiver. "Your jacket," Joel murmured. He held it for her and it was only then that she sensed how tense he was. It made Tiffany even more miserable to think how relieved he would be when this parting was finally over.

He accompanied her down the gangplank, past the security guards, who stood aside respectfully. Joel paused momentarily to issue a command to the two men. "No one is to leave the yacht until I get back. And I mean no one...for any reason!"

They "yes-sirred" with vigour.

Joel Faber undoubtedly felt forced to ensure that she got away safely, but Tiffany knew she couldn't allow him to do that. No way would he appreciate the fact that Garret McKeogh had brought her here in his boat.

She had to keep the rendezvous with the fishing trawler private.

As soon as they were off the jetty she slowed her pace, intending to send Joel back before they reached the hotel. A glance at her watch showed she still had half an hour before she had to be at the pier.

"I appreciate that you had to think fast to get us out of the mess I caused you," she remarked ruefully. "But I take it nothing's really changed. And please don't think I expect anything from you. I understand why you said what you did."

He threw her a dark unreadable look. "Don't you realise we have to follow through?"

She paused in her step, disturbed by the undertone of savagery in his voice. The pressure of his hand on the pit of her back kept her moving.

"We're being watched," he reminded her.

Tiffany was plunged into turmoil, even as she obeyed the necessity to keep walking in a purposeful manner. Although she certainly wanted Joel Faber's help, the idea of his being blackmailed into it did not sit well with her. And it was all her fault!

"I'm sorry," she whispered. "Can't you simply say you've changed your mind? Or —"

"Are you prepared to give up on Haven Bay?" he cut in pointedly.

"I can't!"

"Then there's no other choice but to work your documentary through Q2RV. If you go elsewhere, Nerida Bellamy will be on to it like a leech. You saw what she's like. She'll figure I lied because I have something to hide. She'll end up grubbing around at Haven Bay, and the way her mind works..."

His jawline tightened as though he were clenching his teeth. Again Tiffany was made aware that whatever pain there was in his past it went very deep with Joel Faber. And it was something he didn't want uncovered. He sucked in a quick breath, then slowly bit out his solution. "If Nerida goes to Haven Bay, I want her mind concentrated on a possible future happening. I don't want her digging up things that are intensely private to me."

Tiffany shook her head in helpless despair. "I didn't mean to do this to you. Please believe that. I know it's no—"

"What's done is done," he said in bitter resignation. "Let's not waste time on a post-mortem. I'd appreciate your minimising any further damage in the future."

"Of course," she agreed hurriedly. "You can trust me to keep your name out of everything to do with Haven Bay, if that's what you want."

"Just keep it strictly business," he said curtly.

Tiffany sighed to release some of her pent-up feelings. "Tell me how you want to handle it and I'll follow your instructions to the letter," she said, regretting ever having gone to him in the first place. If ever there was a case of fools rushing in where angels feared to tread, this was it.

He didn't answer immediately. She could feel his tension curling around her in choking waves. They stepped off the jetty and headed towards the hotel. While she still had ample time before she had to be at the pier, she certainly didn't have time for a long conversation with Joel Faber. She had to take her leave of him before they reached the hotel, or he would find out she hadn't come by car. And if he learned the real truth of how she had got here, he might think she was in league with Garret against him in some way.

"I can give you my sister's telephone number if you want to think about it," she offered quickly.

"No. I want no further contact with you, Tiffany. Not in any form," he said decisively, a hard cutting edge to his voice. "I'll set up all the authority you'll need with the present management at Q2RV. That's half-done already. I'll make it official on Monday. You can take it from there. Use whatever resources you want. Make your documentary. Choose what you consider is the most favourable airtime. And that finishes it. The film will be yours. You can hawk it to any network that wants it. I want nothing more to do with it. I want nothing more to do with you. And I certainly don't want any further involvement with Haven Bay. Is that understood?"

"Yes. Thank you." It was an amazingly generous settlement of the problem, but it was perfectly clear he wanted no argument about it. And perfectly clear that any personal connection to Haven Bay was total anathema to him.

She stopped walking and faced him, sick at the thought of leaving him like this, but knowing she had no other choice. "You needn't come any further with me, Joel. There's no more to say, is there?"

He made no move to urge her on this time. They were out of sight from the yacht, and no one had followed them. The dim lighting along the path to the hotel left his face in shadow, but the taut lines of it were clear enough. His features could have been carved from granite. Tiffany felt rather than saw or heard the pain behind his reply.

"No. It's too late to change...anything. Garret brought you, didn't he? I saw you arrive on the trawler."

Tiffany swallowed the shock of this bald statement, and knew that there could be no deception. Although she would have liked to deny it, for his sake, he was demanding the truth and she gave it.

"Yes. Garret brought me. But he didn't think I'd get to you," she answered simply.

He gave a harsh laugh, and his head jerked in a negative movement. "You got to me. He succeeded. Of course he would have been planning this from the moment you gave him the opening.''

''Why do you say that?'' she asked, wondering if it was true. Had old Garret suggested Joel Faber first, or had she? What *was* behind it all? ''What do you mean?'' she pressed more urgently when Joel ignored her question.

''It has nothing to do with you,'' he said in curt dismissal. ''Leave it alone. Get on with whatever it is you have to do, for your sister and her son, and yourself. Now go!''

''I'll never see you again, will I?''

''No! Never!''

She stood staring up at him, unable to bring herself to walk away even though she knew it was what he wanted. And what she had wanted herself a little while ago. But now that the time of parting was upon her, somehow it seemed terribly wrong. She had felt at that first moment of meeting that their paths had always been destined to intersect somewhere, sometime, but surely not just for this one night.

''Do you think that's right?'' she asked, tentatively putting her feeling into words.

"Yes!" he replied unequivocally. Then she sensed a slight softening in him. His mouth tilted in gentle mockery. "I doubt that it would do either of us any good to meet again. And oddly enough, I prefer you not to be hurt through me." He lifted his hand and touched her cheek in a brief salute. "Goodbye, Tiffany James."

He turned and strode away from her, back to his yacht, back to his lonely glittering world, back to the barricade of cynicism with the inner despair that nothing could reach.

And Tiffany could not stop the tears that welled into her eyes. She wanted to beat down the barricade, take away the despair, satisfy the hunger...but she could not, in all decency, inflict herself on him again. Yet he left her with a feeling of loss that dragged at her own soul.

She dashed the trickling tears away with the back of her hand. Armand's ring scraped against her eyebrow. She lowered her hand, staring down at the ring that had contributed its fateful twist to events. Pearls for tears, she thought, and wrenched it off her finger.

All men were not fickle, she told herself sternly. She was not going to let her thinking be warped by one incident in her life, however hurtful it had been. From now on she was only going to remember the good times with Armand, and she slid the ring on to the third finger of her right hand. There was a long future stretching ahead of her. And it was always possible that her path would cross Joel Faber's again in more auspicious circumstances, when she was no longer so closely involved with the place he hated so much.

She suddenly realised that Joel Faber had taken two decisions out of her hands tonight. The promotion for Haven Bay was now set and would have to go ahead. Which might be a good thing. Maybe if she could produce a great success, some other big developer would become interested in making the large investment required. In any event, Carol and Alan would be delighted at the news that some move on the future was about to be made.

And old Garret could think on Joel Faber's generosity, because Tiffany wasn't going to tell him anything else about their meeting. If the old fisherman *had* used her for some dark nefarious purpose of his own, he would get no satisfaction from her. Joel Faber wanted the past left in the past. She owed him that at the very least.

As she headed for the end of the pier to wait for the trawler, Tiffany deliberately turned her mind to the future. She felt an urgency about getting things done now, and there were dozens of things to be organised before the documentary went to air. She would have to get the whole community working on it straight away. Postcards, souvenirs, extra stocks of films for cameras, parking areas to be set aside, schedules to be drawn up for the trawler trips.

And since she had been given a totally free hand to make any kind of documentary she wished, backed by all the resources at Q2RV, Tiffany reckoned she could produce a special-interest show that might very well have viewers clamouring for more. And what would Joel Faber do about that? It was certainly possible that any contact between them might not be at an end, after all!

# CHAPTER SIX

THE PERVERSITY of human nature was a marvellous thing, Tiffany reflected over the next few weeks. The news that Joel Faber was prepared to back the tourist enterprise to the tune of footing the bill for the documentary, which would be given the best possible exposure, brought a curious range of reactions, particularly from the older members of the Haven Bay community.

"So he ought!" Garret muttered darkly. "It's well past time he gave something back for what he took."

When Tiffany asked what he meant by that, the old fisherman just shook his head and held his silence.

However, other residents expressed surprise, even puzzlement that Joel Faber would want to do anything at all for Haven Bay. Any suggestion of sentimentality towards his old hometown was dismissed out of hand. The way Reuben had raised him and worked him, Joel Faber had never had any reason to like anything about the place. And then the storm...heads were shaken in silent, knowing accord. The only answer they could come up with was that the tourist idea must be a good one and Joel Faber would do anything for money. On that score agreement was reached.

The important result of this conclusion was that the ingrained conservatism of Haven Bay's senior citizens, who had viewed Tiffany's idea for a tourism industry with absolute pessimism, began to give way to a more hopeful and positive participation in the scheme. After all, Joel Faber knew what he was about. He had proved himself a shrewd businessman over and over again. He wouldn't have come into this project unless there was something in it for him. It had to be a good idea.

Since belief in a cause was half the battle, Tiffany said nothing to correct this mistaken conclusion. For the scheme to work well it needed everyone pulling together. Because she had absolute faith in it herself, she saw no reason to reveal that Joel Faber's private and almost certainly prejudiced opinion of the whole idea was distinctly unfavourable.

Confidence rubbed off on the business people of the town, who were the main money investors in the project. They stopped talking about risks and started speculating about profits. Idea built on idea. A camping ground was set aside. Facilities were built. Shopkeepers reassessed and increased their stock supplies. Progress meetings became the main social activity of the village.

There never had been any problem in enthusing the younger generation with the scheme. It was their future. They had nothing to lose and everything to gain. But most of all, it carried a sense of adventure that excited and enthused them. They were ready and willing to take up the challenge. Trawlers were slipped and refurbished and repainted until they gleamed. Signs were made for the benefit of visitors. Bunting decorated the streets. Slowly the village of Haven Bay began to change, superficially at least.

Alan was to be the booking agent, roustabout and general factotum. Initially it would be in partnership with Tiffany, but once he had left school at the end of the year he was to take over and run everything himself, with the ready help of his mother as general secretary and treasurer. Tiffany rented a small shop in the main street for his office. It had been abandoned years ago and needed a lot of fixing up. Alan's school friends pitched in to help. The walls were scrubbed and painted, and an art student painted a mural of whales on the walls.

Now that her anxiety about Alan's future was taking on a new dimension, Carol was a whirlwind of happy activity. Her Vietnamese background had been viewed with mistrust and suspicion by the villagers when she first came to town. Her ways were the ways of the foreigner. But she had won them over with her unfeigned naturalness, her dedication to hard work and to making a success of her life and Alan's. Of course, the way both mother and son had determinedly risen above their handicaps could do nothing else but earn respect and admiration. They had long ceased being foreigners and were simply people who had been dealt a raw deal by life.... A fine example to everyone that a life could be made worth living no matter what.

For some years now Carol had served as a teaching aide at the Haven Bay school, and she had no trouble rallying the headmaster and staff into starting a community-conscious programme. So successful was it that at weekends the schoolchildren formed working bees to clean up around the village. Fences were painted, lawns mowed, gardens spruced up, rubbish collected and disposed of. A very real sense of community pride was quickly generated.

Now that she had stirred Haven Bay out of its apathy, it was up to Tiffany to deliver! The documentary was the keystone to the whole operation. Tiffany expanded her initial half-hour idea to a full-blown hour programme and decided on a prime-time Sunday evening slot. The Q2RV news broadcast would lead into it, and the one really popular show on Q2RV, a comedy hour, would follow it.

She had decided on two thirty-second trailers to promote the documentary and tease viewers' interest. Tiffany would have liked to do more, but there had to be a limit to what Joel Faber would tolerate, and she expected she had just about reached it already. Apart from which, she had told him the only cost would be the film, which was true, more or less.

It took Tiffany much longer than she expected to write the script to her satisfaction. Then, with mounting trepidation, she rang her brother, Zachary Lee. She couldn't control the butterflies in her stomach as the imminent time of decision grew closer. No one in their right mind wouldn't have had qualms about what could happen. Tiffany wondered if she was in her right mind to have taken this venture on, but she couldn't afford the time to pursue that train of thought to a rigorous logical conclusion.

Zachary Lee was totally supportive and threw in a few ideas to help. He was sending a team of cameramen—no, he'd changed his mind—he was *bringing* a team of cameramen. This was a time for family to stick together. He was behind Tiffany all the way. Alan deserved the best possible shot at this venture.

A warm wave of reassurance swept through Tiffany. Zachary Lee James would make sure the documentary was a winner. He had an especially soft spot for Carol and Alan. He had helped smuggle them out of Vietnam, so horrified by their plight that he had had no patience with government rules and red tape.

He had been a television reporter then, covering the war, and not even the horrors he had seen had blunted his deep compassion or the essential gentleness of his nature. He was a big man, this brother of hers, Tiffany thought proudly. And not just in physique, although he dwarfed most people around him. He was big in every way.

They set down Wednesday for the day; it would be relatively quiet, and Tiffany prayed it wouldn't rain. She wanted a glorious fine day that would display Haven Bay at its best.

The Fates were not that kind. The barometer dropped rapidly on Tuesday night, and the meteorological report was for a cold front that had come all the way from the Antarctic, across the Indian Ocean, along the Great Australian Bight, had forced its way through Bass Strait and would hit with moderate to strong winds and heavy rain the next day. It was the last thing Tiffany wanted. She rang Zachary Lee to tell him to cancel.

He laughed softly down the telephone. "No, Sis." The gentle American accent he had never quite lost gave a soft sibilance to his voice. "This time you're wrong. Drama. That's what we've got. That's what we're going to give them. Trust me. It will work. I can always take the good shots to round the story off. What we have here is nature. NATURE in capital letters at its wildest and furious best. And Haven Bay is relatively protected. Let's show people the difference, these mighty creatures of the sea in their *real* element. After all, if tourists are coming, Tiff, every day is not a fine day. Show the truth!''

Tiffany sighed and threw away her script. This was a completely new ballgame. She rang up Garret and alerted him that, come hell or high water, tomorrow they were going ahead full steam. Zachary Lee James had said so.

When Zachary Lee's team arrived the next morning, it was as if Haven Bay had declared a public holiday. No one wanted to miss out on watching the making of the documentary. Not even the heavy squalls of rain deterred them from taking up vantage positions around the harbour. In actual fact, the stormy weather had brought more whales into the bay than usual, and excitement ran high as the television men loaded all their technical gear on to Garret's trawler, the *Southern Cross*. The helicopter that had brought them was sent up to take overhead shots, for which the voice-over would be done later. A fine introductory segment, Tiffany thought.

Alan, of course, accompanied them on the trawler. She had rehearsed him for one interview, Garret for another, but the whales and Haven Bay were the real stars. They shot one awesome sequence of a huge humpback and her calf dipping through the crashing waves, spray flying everywhere, and only a few metres from the boat. Tiffany ended up doing an impromptu interview with one of the cameramen, who was almost beside himself with excitement.

"Fantastic! Unbelievable!" he kept saying. "I've shot film all over the world. I've been to Kathmandu and Timbuktu. I've been through wars and to trouble spots and all the godforsaken places on the globe. I didn't think there was anything else to see or learn. But I've never experienced anything like this. To be so close to such a mighty creation of nature...it makes you feel...it's inexpressible...humbling, uplifting." He shook his head, but the expression on his face said it all. "No one should miss seeing it. No one!"

The footage they shot that day was wild and wonderful. Watching these Goliaths of the ocean surging through their element, oblivious to the power of nature—it *was* exhilarating, uplifting! Tiffany felt sure that no viewer could fail to be thrilled by it. By the time they arrived back on shore, they were all saturated, despite their oilskins, shivering cold and ravenously hungry. Carol had steaming pots of tea and coffee ready for them, and enough of her special lamb stew to feed everyone twice over. It was a blissful aftermath, with the sense of sharing that Tiffany could only liken to a blitz mentality.

She was totally exhausted. How Zachary Lee had got all these people to contribute their time and effort for nothing she didn't know. But there was not a word about costs, not even for the helicopter. And they all came back for another shoot the following week. It was completely uneventful. The sense of excitement and sharing was gone. This was just a professional job, professionally done. There was a final interview with Alan and Carol to focus the story on human beings. Then all that had to be accomplished was the editing process that would fit it all together in the kind of theme that would sell Haven Bay to the public.

Carol's small fragile frame was almost lost in Zachary Lee's farewell bear hug. No two people could ever look less like brother and sister, Tiffany thought, but the bond was there, as strong as any bloodline; the bond of caring. Alan looked up at the big man with the bright chestnut hair and the soft hazel eyes and his own dark eyes shone with sheer adoration. No matter what Zachary Lee ever did, he would always be a hero to Alan.

Tiffany flew back to Sydney with her brother and conferred over the final product. Since Joel Faber had waived all future rights to it, Zachary Lee was to show the documentary on his television station a week after Q2RV, then negotiate deals with other networks in Australia, the U.S.A. and Japan. Tiffany lined up special promotions with the big travel agencies. She had one message and one message only—promote, promote, promote. She was determined to draw overseas tourists as well as get a good foot on the home market. Everyone was grist to her mill.

Tiffany hoped she had not overlooked anything. It was so critical that every possible preparation be considered and taken care of.

The next step was the lead-up publicity for the show itself. The management at Q2RV was most co-operative. The fiction that her documentary was a pilot show to test ratings was still very much in force, and Tiffany had no compunction about using the leverage that gave her.

She was granted favourable time slots for the thirty-second trailers. They were to be played every evening throughout the lead-up week. Special advertisements for the show were inserted in newspapers and magazines. Somehow she never got around to querying how this was happening, or who was paying for it.

The critical Sunday finally came. As Tiffany drove in to Q2RV to monitor the viewer reaction—if there was any—she hoped that as many television sets everywhere else would be tuned in to the show as in Haven Bay. The fever of anticipation in the village was so high it made Tiffany feel nervous. *But whatever happens,* she told herself, *we did our best.*

The mood at Q2RV was taut with expectancy, whether for success or failure Tiffany wasn't quite sure. She was, after all, an outsider, and she couldn't very well assure the people who worked there that she wasn't going to affect their lives in any way, even if the documentary should prove a great hit with viewers. The knowledge that this was the end as far as Joel Faber was concerned was for herself alone.

Tiffany's nervousness left her as the show started. It was good. She was certain it was better than good. Compelling. Surely no one who had started to watch it would switch off. She wondered if Joel Faber was watching. She hoped he was. Maybe it would help distance the past from the present and make him see things differently. If only he would swing his weight and expertise into a tourist industry at Haven Bay, Tiffany was sure that possibilities would fast become probabilities.

She didn't have to wait long for the viewer reaction. No sooner had the documentary rolled its final credits than the Q2RV switchboard lit up with calls. The telephone number of the booking agency at Haven Bay was requested so many times that the station flashed it on to the screen throughout the rest of the evening's programmes. There was no doubting that the show had stirred enormous interest.

A personal call came through for Tiffany, and her heart leaped at the thought it might be Joel Faber. Her disappointment melted into a smile as she heard the distinctive voice of her brother. Zachary Lee had rung to congratulate her.

"You were marvellous, Sis, even if I say so myself."

"You're biased, prejudiced, and it was all your skill," she said, laughing back at him.

"Tiff, it was your idea. In our job, ideas are the red blood cells of life. They carry the oxygen of survival."

She heaved a sigh as the word *survival* brought Joel Faber to mind again. It might be extremely stupid of her, but she didn't want this to be the end of any association between them. Somehow it wasn't right. Couldn't be right.

"Well, all we can do now is wait and see if it works out," she said to Zachary Lee.

"That's right, Sis. Wait and see," he replied in the soft manner that reflected the inner qualities of her brother: the calmness, gentleness, serenity always so surprising in such a big man.

"Thanks for ringing," she said warmly.

"Always a pleasure, Tiff. Let me know if there's any more I can do to help."

And the wonderful thing was that Tiffany knew that Zachary Lee meant it. The family never failed to help when or how or if it could. She felt a deep well of compassion for people who had no family. Like Joel Faber. And old Garret. The lack of it had obviously turned them in on themselves.

If success could be measured by the number of enquiries at the booking agency the next day, then the documentary had been a roaring triumph. Haven Bay was about to be swamped by visitors. The telephone never stopped ringing. Tiffany was mightily relieved that their preparations for this eventuality had been so thorough. The camping ground was booked out for the following weekend. They couldn't actually provide all the accommodation that was asked of the few guest houses available. The scheduling of trawler trips had to be upgraded to satisfy demand. The village of Haven Bay was galvanised into action to meet the onslaught of tourists that was no longer a possibility but a fast-approaching reality.

Sightseers started coming during the week. The village was ready for them, but the first weekend was almost bedlam. Crowds poured in on Saturday. Day-trippers who hadn't booked ahead for the trawler trips were inevitably disappointed, but they seemed reasonably content to walk up to the bluff that overlooked all the activity. At least they could see the whales from a distance. The villagers rallied to meet their needs, setting up food stalls in the streets to sell sandwiches, hot dogs and drinks.

A news team from Q2RV arrived, and Haven Bay was featured on television again that night, along with the more exciting segments from the documentary. The crowds were even bigger on Sunday. Among the influx of visitors was the society reporter, Nerida Bellamy, who ran Tiffany to ground in the booking agency in much the same way as she had cornered Joel Faber that night on the yacht.

''Television or tourism—which is your area of expertise, Miss James?'' she demanded archly.

Tiffany smiled as disarmingly as she could. "Both," she replied.

The woman's return smile was all sabre-toothed tiger. "Which makes you an extremely compatible . . . partner for Joel Faber. You're fronting for him here, aren't you? He's testing the waters before plunging in on a new tourist development. It's all been a double game, hasn't it?"

The irony of the situation made Tiffany's voice very dry. "I wouldn't call it a game. As far as I'm concerned, it's serious business. And as far as Joel Faber's future intentions are concerned, you'll have to ask him."

Nerida's sharp blue eyes narrowed. "Since he's been incommunicado since his yacht party, you are well aware that he's made it impossible for me to ask him anything. But he can hardly stay in that fortress home of his on Leisure Island forever. So don't think you can keep fooling me, Miss James. Sooner or later you'll get together again. And I'll be waiting. And watching."

"Why?" Tiffany asked curiously. She really wanted to know what drove this woman to be such a bloodhound.

The woman gave her a venomous look. "Because, my dear Miss James, I don't believe either of you. And I intend to be proved right."

That was the crux of it, Tiffany suddenly realised. The woman hated to be proved wrong, particularly in public. Tiffany wondered how many times Joel Faber had proved Nerida wrong. Certainly the reporter had the bit between the teeth where he was concerned, and she was not going to let go until she had something on him.

It wouldn't be Haven Bay, Tiffany thought ruefully. She wished Joel Faber would change his mind about helping this particular tourist industry along, and change his mind about other things, too, but unless something happened to make him do so he was not about to backpedal on his edict. No further contact, he'd said. Yet there had been that note of regret in his voice when she had challenged his decision. He couldn't really want to be left alone. No one really wanted to be alone.

"That fortress home..." Why had he been blocking out the rest of the world since her meeting with him? The question teased Tiffany for a considerable length of time. Joel

Faber obviously needed to be dragged back to the human race. Whether he liked it or not. She would even ignore his contempt of do-gooding if she could do some good for him.

TWO WEEKS LATER, Tiffany was presented with a situation in which she had no choice. Haven Bay had fast become a *must* visit for tourists. Boat activity in the area had become so hectic that the navy had sent a coastguard vessel to patrol the waters in order to protect the whales from interference from outsiders who were not familiar with the huge crea-tures' habits. The village itself was under-going such a change of pace that everyone was caught between exhaustion and exhilaration. The bank manager was wearing the kind of smile unseen in the whole twenty years he had been stationed there. And then came the first big step towards international recognition.

A travel agent telephoned to say an entire Boeing 747 had been booked by Qantas in Japan. People were coming en masse to see the whales. It was the first confirmation that Haven Bay had hit the big time, and Tiffany's mind momentarily reeled at the thought that a full flight was being organised around *her* tourist project. It literally took her breath away.

"We can't fit them in!" Despair was in Alan's voice and eloquently written on his fine Eurasian face. The enormity of what he was telling her was too much for him. For once he moved awkwardly on his artificial legs, as if he had never mastered them, and collapsed into a chair, his shoulders drooping in desperate disappointment.

"Book it!" Tiffany commanded.

His eyes were dark pools of defeat. "There are no boats left. There is nothing left to juggle."

"Book it!"

"We can't do it! The people we've booked are flying in, traveling thousands of miles."

"Book it!"

He shook his head. "You can't mean that, Aunt Tiff."

"I do."

He finally acknowledged the determined purpose on her face. "What are you going to do?"

"I'll find a way."

Alan took the booking. Tiffany could see the reluctance in his manner, the fear that it would all go wrong. He had no conviction that Tiffany could do anything at all. He was certain that she had done something utterly stupid. Tiffany wondered if she had.

The next few days certainly indicated that she had promised more than she could deliver. Try as they might, they could not beg, borrow, lease, buy or steal the boat space they needed. And they had five hundred Japanese tourists coming to see the whales.

Slowly the idea dawned. There was one possibility left. Tiffany repressed a *frisson* of horror at her own temerity. But there was no other way... at least that she could think of. Besides, if he was living like a recluse in his home at Leisure Island, he wasn't using his yacht. *Liberty* was undoubtedly docked at its jetty in the marina, completely idle. Which, under the circumstances, was a tragedy. Its crew really should be doing something to earn whatever wages they were paid. And it wouldn't hurt Joel Faber to lend it to her just this once.

After all, she had proof enough to make him eat his words about Haven Bay anyway. Not only had the documentary scored the highest ratings Q2RV had ever had, but the show had even been repeated by popular demand. He could not deny that the old fishing village had received a shot in the arm of massive proportions. His prophecy of disaster was clearly false. Haven Bay was not about to lie down and die, and Joel Faber might as well face that fact. It might even do him some good.

But this time, before confronting him again, she was going to get some straight facts out of old Garret. Something had happened twenty years ago, something that hadn't been laid to rest. Something more than the storm, and it deeply involved both men. She couldn't go to Joel Faber in ignorance a second time. Too much had been said, too much implied. The only way to reach in to him was if she was armed with understanding.

# CHAPTER SEVEN

"I'M GOING TO ASK Joel Faber for the use of his yacht," Tiffany told the old fisherman point-blank.

Garret McKeogh stared at her, his expression totally inscrutable. He was well aware of the problem they had on their hands. "Do you need me to take you to him?" he asked after a heavy silence.

"No. You're going flat out with the tourists, so you haven't got the time. I'll have to make it on my own," Tiffany told him. She suspected that Garret's help the first time had been a weighing factor in Joel Faber's decision to have no further contact with her. She wasn't going to make that mistake twice. "I need you to tell me what happened on the day of the storm," she said, her kingfisher-blue eyes fixed on his with determined purpose.

"It's gone!" he countered brusquely.

"You remember," Tiffany replied with pointed emphasis. "All the old-timers remember. I want to know why they won't speak of it. I need to know, Garret. It stands in my way of progress now. I know that from my last meeting with Joel Faber...and you know it, too."

Indecision wavered across his face. His eyes avoided hers. His reply was gruff. "No one wants to drag up those memories. Too many people died that night. Died uselessly. Died unnecessarily. I told them what would happen. And it did. It did," he repeated grimly.

"What happened exactly? I know it was some kind of rescue attempt," Tiffany prompted quickly.

"Aye." He nodded, his eyes flashing contempt. "But there was not a hope in hell that it could be successful. And no one should have been out in that storm. There'd been warning enough on the radio. We found out later that the yacht that sent up the distress signals was crewed by amateurs who had gone out against all advice. Headstrong fools! Not worth saving, putting others' lives at risk."

"And they died?"

"Aye. And deserved to," old Garret said with unrelenting condemnation. "The yacht went down before the first trawler had got anywhere near it. Then one of the trawlers foundered, and Reuben Faber went to its rescue. Madness, it was. But there was never any stopping Reuben when he made up his mind. Mad, he was. Mad, they all were. And they all died."

His mouth thinned into the grizzled beard, and the steel-grey eyes flashed with some strong emotion. "All except him."

"Joel?" Tiffany asked, her heart leaping in hope for some insight.

"Aye. The devil was on his side," the old man confirmed with an edge of bitterness. "The only one who was washed up alive."

"And do you hate him for that, Garret?" she put softly.

He gave her a basilisklike stare—cold, hard, bleak, drained of all life. "It's too long ago to hate anyone," he said at last, his voice flat and dull.

Tiffany didn't have to be told he would say no more on the subject. He had closed up on her again. Still, she felt she had a glimmer of understanding now. She remembered that strong first impression she had of Joel Faber, the survivor against all odds, with no joy in him.

She wondered how it felt to be a survivor when everyone else had died. To be the only one. To feel other people looking at you and perhaps wishing it had been someone dearer to them who had come back alive. Had it been simple luck that he didn't drown like the rest? Or had he been the strongest one, the smartest one, the one who hung on when everyone else let go? Had the villagers made him feel guilty for not dying? Was that why nobody wanted to talk about it? Was that why Joel Faber would be glad to see Haven Bay die?

But it was twenty years ago, Tiffany protested silently. As Garret said, too long ago to hate, although she wasn't sure that the old fisherman had spoken the absolute truth on that score. Nevertheless she thanked him for having told her what he had.

As she could find out nothing more, Tiffany implemented her decision to go and find Joel Faber. After his determination to cut all future contact between them, it was useless to think of telephoning him. She had to do what she had done before, reach him any way she could, even if she was unwelcome and unannounced.

She borrowed Garret's small runabout boat and gave herself the morning to motor up to Leisure Island. If Joel Faber was really hiding in his fortress home, as Nerida had said, the sea was again the obvious line of approach. The sun had passed its zenith by the time Tiffany had located his private retreat. It was situated above a sheltered little cove on the north side of the island. A high security fence marked its boundaries, and she was relieved to see a jetty running out from a private beach. This was protected from the worst of the elements by the fingerlike protrusion of a small peninsula.

Tiffany passed a few vessels anchored in the miniharbour, but they ignored her and she ignored them. She cut the engine of the small outboard motor and coasted in on the blind side of a speedboat that was tied to Joel's jetty. No one came to stop her. As far as she could tell, her arrival was completely unobserved.

Tiffany ran lightly up the jetty, calculating her next move. Her eyes were trained on the path leading from the beach to the house. She only just saw the man in time before com-

mitting herself to the course of action she had
in mind. It brought her to an instant halt.

He was lying on the sand, apparently sun-
bathing. Obviously he was no security guard.
He appeared to be asleep, stretched out on his
stomach, his head turned away from her.

Tiffany kept an eye on him for any
movement, but there was none. Which was
just as well, because he was obviously intent
on getting an all-over tan. As far as she could
see he was stark naked. In his present situation, a confrontation could only embarrass
both of them.

Tiffany was inwardly debating how best to
get past him when the unnerving suspicion
crossed her mind that this man was Joel Faber
himself. The black hair, the length of him, the
lean muscularity of his physique... If he was
the man she sought—and the suspicion was
growing stronger every moment—it would be
a waste of time to go up to the house.

She took a deep breath. With her pulse gal-
loping at every step, she moved stealthily
along the wet edge of the sand, not wanting
to waken him until she had got a good look
at his face and was certain who he was.

It was he all right. There was no mistaking the distinctive cut of his hard hungry features. Tiffany stood stock-still for several minutes, studying him, wondering how best to deal with the situation. Her heart was thumping in agitation. For some reason she found his nakedness very disturbing now that she knew it was *his* nakedness. And she certainly hadn't planned on this happening to her.

His body had a sleek dangerous look about it, powerful muscles now relaxed under the sheen of sun-bronzed skin, but ready to spring into virile movement at a moment's warning. He probably wasn't going to like being caught like this. Not by her. Yet she couldn't just walk away. Somehow she had to turn this opportunity into an advantage so that he would not turn her away. However, it did require gentle handling.

A discarded pair of shorts lay near his feet. Tiffany very quietly picked them up, then sat down on the sand a few feet away from him, in his direct line of vision when he opened his eyes. She put his shorts behind her so he couldn't see them. When she felt calm enough to proceed, she picked up a little pebble and lobbed it on to the pit of his back. It wasn't until the third pebble bounced off his shoulder and struck his cheek that he frowned in irritation. The fourth pebble opened his eyes.

"Hello again," she said, very softly, needing to draw his attention without jolting him into any abrupt movement.

He didn't move. He stared into her eyes with an oddly glazed look for several moments before his focus sharpened with recognition. His face tightened, then relaxed into a sardonic little smile. "You are full of surprises, Tiffany James."

The low drawl seemed to slide into Tiffany's stomach and stirred a host of butterflies. But at least he didn't sound hostile toward her. "I'm sorry for waking you up, but I need to talk to you," she said apologetically.

"Well, how about that!" he mocked, and drew his arms to prop himself on his elbows. His gaze took in the details of her appearance: her long honey-blonde hair piled up into a casual topknot, the loose white shirt with its ends tied in a knot at her waist, the wide-legged white shorts that ended mid-thigh, the long tanned length of her legs, the sneakers on her feet. "You're starting to make this a habit,'' he said with a trace of dry whimsy.

Tiffany tore her own gaze away from the muscles now so sharply delineated in his arms, his shoulders, his back, the taut cheeks of his buttocks. "You need a towel. Or some clothes. I could get them for you, if you're nice to me."

He grinned at her, a most unwholesome wickedness dancing through his amusement.

It wasn't the heat of the sun that tingled under Tiffany's skin. This encounter wasn't starting as she had planned. In fact, she had a very hot feeling it was about to go awfully awry. However, at least he wasn't angry with her for coming to him, despite his edict.

She smiled, fighting to keep a calm composure. "I came by myself this time. I tied up at your jetty. And now I'm saving you from getting very badly burnt. Don't you know it's dangerous to go to sleep on the beach?"

"I guess I like being dangerous." His eyes suddenly glittered with the hungry desire she had been so aware of at their first meeting. "Too many sleepless nights," he mused softly, "and now you're here."

He shifted, his hand shooting out to fasten around her wrist. Before Tiffany realised his intention, she was pulled off balance and landed flat on her back on the sand. He had her pinned there, his face hovering directly over hers as she struggled to get her breath back. It was extremely difficult with his bare chest resting lightly on her breasts.

"That wasn't fair!" she accused as a treacherous turbulence raced through her.

"Who cares?" Satisfaction gleamed down at her, unholy satisfaction. "You caught me at a disadvantage. Or so you thought. I simply changed the rules. Who knows where this might lead? Don't you think it's only fair if you're naked, too?"

Her heart catapulted between her throat and her stomach. Her voice came out in little strangled chokes. "Joel. No. I didn't mean to bargain with you. I didn't want to upset you. But you make it so hard for me to come to you. I didn't expect . . . I didn't know what to do."

A guttural sound of disapproval added to the chaos inside her head. He bent his head and his lips tingled temptingly over hers. "Why shouldn't I kiss you?" he murmured.

"Why shouldn't I take what I want? You use me for your wants, Tiffany. You do as you like. You invade my privacy, my dreams."

Dreams? Had she been on his mind as much as he had been on hers? What kind of dreams? Good? Bad? Haunting memories of the storm at Haven Bay? Perhaps it wasn't fair of her to come back to him, no matter what the reason.

Her wild thoughts became a meaningless jumble as his mouth grazed over her lips. His tongue traced an exquisite line of pleasure as he searched for what he would devour. Danger shrieked through Tiffany's mind. If he kissed her as he had before with that terrible ravaging passion...

"Don't!" she gasped, jerking her head aside. "Please, Joel...no! I have to ask a favour of you and it can't be done like this," she blurted out in desperation.

"Then let this be your favour to me," he demanded harshly.

Her eyes sought his in disbelief. "You don't mean that, Joel."

"Perhaps not." The bitter cynicism that swirled down at her gradually subsided into dark soul-weariness. He closed his eyes against the frantic appeal in hers and shook his head. "You shouldn't have come back, Tiffany. You stir a hunger, a need in me, that I would rather forget. Go now. Go while you are safe."

While those words were still sinking into her disordered mind, he let her go and rolled away from her. Tiffany pushed herself up into a sitting position, feeling totally at odds with herself. He had made it eminently clear that she shouldn't have come, yet she couldn't make herself get to her feet and go. Apart from the fact she felt appallingly shaky, she also felt a need for him in some helplessly tangled way.

She picked up his shorts and tossed them to him. "I want to talk to you," she pleaded, her voice filled with a thousand uncertainties. "Can't you just talk with me?"

His eyes warred sharply with hers, then retreated into grim mockery. He rose to his feet as if to show her his total unconcern at being found naked by her. The wayward thought ran through Tiffany's mind that he was far more impressively built than Armand. Then he turned his back to her and drew on the shorts.

For several nerve-stretching moments he stood quite still, apparently watching one of the vessels anchored out beyond the jetty, or perhaps making up his mind whether to stay with her or walk away. Tiffany didn't even think of trying another appeal. Her whole being was concentrated on willing him to give her more time.

Finally he sat down, but made no physical or verbal acknowledgment of her presence. He leaned forward, hunching over his drawn-up knees, his face turned broodingly out to sea. There was a strange intimacy in the silence that locked them together, not touching, but intensely aware of each other.

"Why didn't you tell me all the story about Carol and Alan?" he asked at last, not turning his head, the muscles in his back tightening as he waited for her answer.

He had watched the documentary, Tiffany realised with a warm rush of pleasure. "You weren't interested, Joel," she reminded him gently.

He bent forward, scooped up a handful of sand and watched it trickle slowly through his fingers. Tiffany wondered if he was interested now, if he felt any compassion for her adopted sister and nephew. They were survivors, like himself. Only they had been scarred by more horror than Joel Faber had ever seen or experienced.

"What happened to Alan's legs?"

It was a flat question, revealing nothing of his thoughts or feelings. But at least there was no shade of that hard cynicism in his voice.

"An antipersonnel mine in Vietnam. He was only two years old at the time. Over there, they call people who are mutilated like that...they call them crabs. It's because of the way they have to move. Carol carried him to an army field hospital where my brother was temporarily stationed. Alan's father was an Australian soldier, but no one wanted them, neither the Vietnamese nor the Australians. All Carol's family was wiped out in a search-and-destroy mission that hit the wrong village. They were the discards of life, at least until Zachary Lee stepped in. Then Mum and Dad took an interest, and there's nothing more to tell. Carol anglicised her name. The trauma of the war made her change a lot of things."

He nodded and scooped up another handful of sand. Tiffany waited, instinctively aware that this was not the time to press anything. The line of communication was too fine, too delicate, too important. A thread of curiosity crept into his next question.

"How did they become your family?"

"Zachary Lee paid a huge bribe to get them on to a boat when Alan was well enough to survive the trip. Our parents claimed them when they reached Darwin. We were well organised. They needed . . . a lot of care."

She paused, uncertain of this ground with Joel Faber, yet the need to gain his understanding clamoured to be met. She took a deep breath and added a further explanation.

"Eventually Alan got artificial legs. They had to be changed frequently as he grew. Carol wanted to settle in a fishing village. It was the closest thing we had to her original home, where she was brought up as a child before the war. But above all, she insisted that Alan never be treated as a cripple. That was important to her, that her son have a full normal life. It was easier to achieve that in a little town than in the city. The problem came later. What kind of future did Alan have at Haven Bay? I guess we all felt we had to do something about it."

He shook his head slowly. Tiffany held her tongue and waited for a comment, but none came. She hoped she hadn't taken the issue too far. After what seemed an aeon of time, he unwound himself and lay back down on the sand, propped on his side, facing her.

Tiffany found herself staring at the tight black curls sprinkled on his chest. Her gaze was inexorably drawn to the dark arrow of hair that disappeared under the waistband of his shorts. She didn't want to meet his eyes. Not until he spoke. Not until he gave her some indication of his inner thoughts.

He reached out and stroked his fingers down her right hand. "You've changed your ring over," he remarked, moving the pearl from side to side in an assessing manner.

"Yes. I should have done it a long time ago. I'm sorry it caused you trouble." The touch of his fingers was sending an electric sensation up her arm. She wondered if she could accept the physical intimacy he was offering, then knew how much he was starting to influence her.

His gaze flicked up and caught hers, his dark eyes sharply probing. "You were engaged to be married?"

She had nothing to hide on that score and replied with direct honesty. "No. I wore it on my left hand as a reminder. A private little misery that I should have dismissed much earlier than I did. I thought, when the ring was given to me, that it meant much more than it did."

"An empty road?" He echoed her own words with a twist of irony.

"Something like that," she agreed.

He nodded and his gaze dropped to the ring again. His fingers trailed away, reluctantly, it seemed. Tiffany kept very still, not knowing what was coming next. She regretted the withdrawal of his gentle touch. For some unaccountable reason she would have liked him to hold her hand.

He rolled a little shell back and forth on the sand, then lifted hooded eyes, his face carefully wiped of any expression. "So tell me what favour you want from me," he said bluntly.

"Nothing that will hurt you. Please believe that. But I do want the loan of *Liberty* for one day. That's all I want," she pleaded softly.

His mouth twitched with amusement. "One day hardly gives you time to cruise to Noumea, even if you are interested in going back to the Club Med. So what do you have on your active little mind?"

Tiffany explained about the Japanese tourists. "I tried every other avenue, Joel," she explained anxiously. "If you can suggest something else, I'll try it. But you must see how important it is not to turn them away."

He nodded, his mouth still playing with a half smile. "I'm the last resort," he concluded.

"Just about," she admitted. "I thought if you weren't using the yacht...we'll pay a hiring fee if you want. Whatever you like."

He shook his head. "I don't want anything from Haven Bay. Certainly not their money. Just tell me which day you need the yacht."

Tiffany hoped that meant he was considering lending it to her, and that it was not preparatory to claiming her nominated day was taken up with other plans. "It's this coming Sunday, Joel. We'd need it there by ten in the morning. That's when the buses should be arriving," she stated matter-of-factly.

"I'll have it there in good time," he said without the slightest hesitation, then smiled sardonically at her shaky sigh of relief. "You really can't run a tourist industry on hope, Tiffany. You've got to be covered every which way. It takes more than good publicity, believe me."

"We're getting better organised all the time," she replied hurriedly. "But things were becoming pretty tight over this. It's very generous of you, Joel. I'm deeply grateful for your help. If there's anything I can do for you..."

Her voice trailed off in face of the mocking gleam in his eyes. The mockery gathered a glitter of amusement as a tide of heat scorched up her throat.

"I know you didn't mean that," he drawled.

"I did. But not..." She faltered again.

"Forget it," he dismissed sharply, as if suddenly impatient with himself.

He dropped his gaze from hers and drew idle squiggles in the sand while Tiffany struggled to regain her composure. She stared down at the squiggles, because looking at any part of his body was infinitely treacherous to any peace of mind.

"I underestimated you," he said musingly, then lifted his eyes in dry acknowledgment. "The documentary you made was a winner in every way."

Her relief at the change of subject was tinged with warm pleasure in his comment. "Zachary Lee was really the driving force behind it," she said, unable to take the credit Joel was giving her. "The wild-weather sequence was his idea."

A whimsical smile played over his lips. "You didn't do the interviews?"

"I was lucky. I happened to be in the right place at the right time."

"Sure. I understand," he drawled. "You were so lucky that you've just stood the industry on its head."

"Something like that," she agreed, smiling at his droll comment.

"How did Zachary Lee become your brother?" Joel asked, the thread of curiosity again creeping into his voice.

"Many years ago, Mum and Dad were in New Orleans, in the United States. Zachary Lee was a whiz at chess. Some unscrupulous people were using him to gamble. He was being forced to hustle his talent. And they abused him if he didn't perform well. He was only seven, and—'' Tiffany suddenly realised this wasn't something ever talked about outside the family. It must sound bizarre to someone else. She shot Joel a look of urgent appeal. ''I shouldn't have told you that. It's very private to Zachary Lee.''

He returned a wry look that had a tinge of sadness. ''Tiffany, I well understand that there are some things a man doesn't want known.''

She instinctively believed this statement. He was speaking from his own heart, and Tiffany fiercely wished he would reveal the dark wounds that had never healed for him. However, it was perfectly clear that he had no intention of doing so.

His face relaxed into an inviting little smile. ''How did you get adopted? Where did you come from?''

Tiffany laughed, glad that he was interested in her. ''I just turned up in a basket in Fiji. An abandoned baby.''

''It doesn't worry you?''

"Why should it? I belong to the greatest family in the world."

His face tightened into a questioning frown. "Don't you wonder who your real parents were?"

"Yes, of course. But it doesn't really matter. The whole human race is just one big family if you stop to think about it."

"I don't think I care to," he said sardonically. "How many more brothers and sisters are there in this family of yours?"

"Only eleven. But it's sort of multi-national."

"Your parents must have been very busy," came the dry comment.

"We were all brought up to look after one another. And we had our chores to do. Mum and Dad encouraged our ambitions and taught us to co-operate. Pulling together, they called it. Pull together and you can conquer anything, they used to say. Pull apart and you're nothing. And being busy isn't a bad thing."

"No." He gave an appreciative smile that added megawatts to his attractiveness. "Not a bad thing at all. It sounds like a good family to be in."

"The best," she said with fervour.

He stared fixedly at her, and she felt rather than saw the deep hunger in him reaching out to her, wanting entry, but not really believing there was any place for him.

"You could belong...if you wanted to, Joel," she said impulsively.

He gave a harsh laugh and the cynicism came sweeping back, closing in the hunger. "Some light-years ago, maybe," he drawled. "It's too late now. And apart from that, there are one or two other problems to solve."

"Like what?"

He waved his hand toward the sea. "One of Nerida Bellamy's minions is out there on a boat with a telephoto lens. Tomorrow you should be on the front pages of one of the tabloids with a headline like 'Secret Love Tryst in the Nude'."

"Oh, no!" Tiffany groaned, appalled that her actions had given that woman more fodder for her nasty brand of reporting.

"Oh, yes!" Joel answered, his mouth curling in distaste.

Her eyes begged his forgiveness. "I swear I didn't mean this to happen."

He gave her an ironic little smile. "If I'd known you were coming, I wouldn't have been in the nude. I did it to show my contempt for such spying. And waking up to see you beside me . . . I'm afraid I forgot about the busy little cameraman until I stood up and saw the boat again."

Tiffany instantly realised it had been a moment of decision about two intrusions in his life, and she had no way of knowing which had influenced the course of action he had followed. It made her feel hollow, deflated. All the time she had been speaking of Carol and Alan, had he been listening at all? Certainly not with the undivided attention she had imagined.

But he had given her the loan of the yacht!

Was that out of some generosity of spirit, or did it fit into some other scheme he had in mind? Tiffany shook her head in confusion and frustration. His cynicism was rubbing off on her and she didn't want it to. Everything about him was influencing her too much. She had to hang on to her own values.

"Does it worry you that they print all these lies?" she asked despondently.

"Apart from the persecution complex, not really," he replied, watching her with that guarded, waiting, weighing look. "I'm not sure how you're going to feel when they photograph you with Alan to show a comparison...."

Revulsion tightened her face. "They wouldn't dare—"

"Anything for sales," he cut in pointedly.

"But...that's obscene!"

"Yes."

He seemed relatively unconcerned. Suspiciously unconcerned. He must have found a way around the problem, Tiffany decided. "What are *you* going to do about it?" she asked.

"I've had a few ideas while we've been talking."

"Such as?"

He didn't answer immediately. Tiffany was suddenly very conscious of a stillness about him. And in that stillness was a tightly coiled tension. Again she was reminded of a savage animal, eyeing its hunter, counting the odds of survival, ready to spring either way. The dark eyes were fixed on hers with intense concentration.

"Once you're married," he started slowly, "all the reporting zest goes out of these things." He paused, then with a studiedly casual shrug, he added, "We could get married."

A weird jolt hit Tiffany's heart. In the next instant, every instinct she had was warning her that this was a trap, deliberately set, and totally fatal. "Be serious!" she snapped, angry that he should try it on her.

One eyebrow rose in quizzical mockery. "Most women would jump at the chance I've just offered you."

"I don't believe you," she scorned. "Most women want to be loved by the man they marry. And you would despise me if I'd jumped at the chance."

"But think of the advantages."

"Stop it, Joel!" Her eyes flashed with contempt for his value judgements. "You're way off-key!"

He heaved a sigh. A shadow of something, perhaps regret, flitted across his face before it relaxed into a matter-of-fact expression. The watchful intensity in his eyes faded to a steady neutral. He spoke in a decisive tone that gave no leeway for protest.

''Since you don't like the idea of being my wife, I'm going to make you *nominal* managing director of Q2RV. The emphasis is on *nominal.* After a month, when the ratings *don't* go up, I'll fire you. Then I'll sell the station. And that will be the end of everything. We can both start again with a clean sheet. A favour for a favour, Tiffany. You get the yacht. I spike Nerida's guns for the umpteenth time.''

Tiffany didn't like it. It was one thing to support a deception for one night, quite another to play at being a nominal managing director for a whole month. Joel Faber was obviously intent on cutting her out of his life. Somehow she felt she had failed. Miserably. It wasn't supposed to end like this. She had tried so hard to reach him, but marrying him would have been impossible. She didn't even know why that cynical offer slid back into her mind. Totally impossible in the circumstances.

The yacht was the important thing. That was what she had come for. If she didn't agree to his plan, she wouldn't get the boat, and Nerida might make some dreadful capital out of this meeting. It wasn't as if Q2RV meant anything to her. If Joel had made up his mind to sell, her being there as nominal managing director wouldn't make a whit of difference. It would be a dreary frustrating month, but she didn't seem to have any real choice about it.

"All right. It's a deal," she agreed.

He regarded her speculatively, as if not sure what she was thinking, or wondering if he could trust her. "It's better this way," he said with an unexpectedly rueful twist. "You're right. I'd make you, or anyone else, a rotten husband."

Then he sprang to his feet and gave her a hand to help her up. "I'll ring the station and make the announcement. Then I'll cross wires with Nerida and interpret her pictures for her. I'll send a car for you on Monday. You shall arrive at Q2RV with all the status that goes with the position. I expect you to carry out your role in the manner to which I've become accustomed. When I'm dealing with you."

"And what's that?" Tiffany asked, trying to ignore the warm grip of his hand on hers.

"With daring and style." His eyes danced mockingly at her as she planted herself on her own two feet in front of him. "And in keeping with that, I'm curious to know what you would have done if I'd refused the yacht. I could have, you know.''

She gave him a rueful smile. ''The very last resort was the navy. I did have it at the back of my mind.''

''The navy?'' he quizzed incredulously.

''They've been most helpful with the coast-guard patrol to protect the whales. And five hundred disappointed Japanese tourists wouldn't be good publicity for the tourist industry in this country. I would have put it to the admiral, as I did before, that this was a matter of national pride and honour. I doubt he would have given me his aircraft carrier, but I think I could have scored a frigate. At the very least, a destroyer. After all, what better purpose does the navy have these days than serving our country when needed?''

He shook his head. ''What alarms me is he might have given it to you. You have one hell of a nerve, Tiffany James.''

''I prefer to think of it as enterprise.''

''Nerve,'' he insisted. ''And almost blind optimism. You play with danger as though it wasn't there. And it is, Tiffany.'' A conflict of interests warred across his face, sharpening the hard angles. His gaze dropped to the hand he was still holding. His thumb pushed roughly at the pearl ring. "You should not be so trusting," he said, then released her hand and waved toward the jetty. "I'd better walk you to your boat."

He set off at a brisk pace as though anxious to be rid of her. Tiffany had to hurry to keep up with him. He asked about the organisational details for Sunday—how many trips out to the whales, how many tourists could be best handled on each trip, what kind of catering was being supplied. He kept the conversation very businesslike right to the point where he threw the mooring rope down to her and there was nothing left for her to do but start the outboard motor.

She looked up at him uncertainly. "Will I see you again, Joel?"

"Not if I can help it," he said with pointed emphasis. Then on a more serious, softer note, he added, "Take care, Tiffany."

And the odd thing was, Tiffany sensed that he did care about her, although he didn't want to. It was all most unsatisfactory. Conscious of the telephoto lens trained on them, she started the motor, gave Joel a brief wave, then headed off around the peninsula and out of sight of the man who didn't want to see her again.

She had a lot of time to ponder over their meeting on the return trip to Haven Bay. Joel Faber was an extremely tantalising man. She knew he was sexually attracted to her, as she was to him. And she reminded him of things he wanted to forget. Somehow she didn't think it was the storm or Haven Bay. Perhaps it was the person he had once been, and that was why he kept saying it was too late, because the course of his life had changed him too much. Or maybe what had happened in the storm had changed him. The more she thought about it, the more confused Tiffany felt, and the more she wanted to meet Joel Faber again.

She wondered what he would do about it if she managed Q2RV in such a way that the ratings went up. He wouldn't have a reason to fire her then. Under those circumstances, he might—he just might—want a great deal more to do with her.

# CHAPTER EIGHT

IT WAS JUST NINE o'clock on Sunday morning when Joel Faber's huge white yacht rounded the bluff and headed into Haven Bay. *Liberty* was such a spectacular sight that tourists and residents lined the harbour wall to watch it come in. The news that Joel Faber had lent his yacht to meet the emergency had sent a wave of relief and elation through the village, and here it was, arriving in good time, cleaving through the water toward them.

Knowing comments were passed around. There was no doubt about it. Joel Faber was gearing up to make a big investment in the Haven Bay tourist industry. Why else would he make sure that nothing went wrong?

Tiffany found this attitude disquieting. To develop a dependency on Joel Faber's supposed backing would be very wrong indeed, yet no matter what she said everyone seemed of the firm opinion that it was only a matter of time before his company declared its intention of commencing a new development.

144

The announcement that she was to be the new managing director of Q2RV hadn't helped this situation, either. The general consensus was that she and Joel Faber were hand in glove. Tourism and television—an unbeatable combination!

Certainly the story in the newspapers had given that impression. Whatever Joel had said to Nerida hadn't entirely clipped her wings. The report included his and Tiffany's association over the Haven Bay documentary, and considerable speculation about the tourist industry that was developing in the wake of it. But no love interest was suggested, and their relationship was laid out as a purely business one. The only photograph used was one that had been taken at the yacht party. The nasty exposure that could have resulted from the meeting with Joel on the beach had been scuttled...but at what cost? Tiffany could only hope that everything would smooth itself out eventually.

"What a super boat!" Alan cried in awed delight as *Liberty* edged in to the deep-water wharf that had been set aside for it. His big dark eyes glowed up at Tiffany. "Wouldn't it be great if we could have the use of it all the time?''

''Alan, this is a one-off situation,'' Tiffany told him sternly. ''We can't count on getting it again, so don't get any wild ideas. Let's keep to the business in hand.''

They went on board as soon as the gangway was in place. Apart from their acting as a small welcoming committee, Alan had the schedules printed out to hand to the captain, and Tiffany wanted to make sure that the crew understood what was required of them. They were courteously escorted to the quarterdeck. Tiffany didn't even see the impressive range of technology that gave the yacht mastery over the elements it was built to withstand. Her gaze locked on to one man and stayed there as he dismissed their escort. The last thing she had expected was to find that the captain was Joel Faber himself.

Sardonic amusement danced back at her. ''Can't you keep away from me, Tiffany?''

He was fully clothed in whites today—in keeping with his status as captain of the yacht—but the image of his naked body with its aggressive masculinity was indelibly stamped on her mind. Before she realised what she was doing, Tiffany was mentally stripping him, which added even more turbulence to her confusion at seeing him. Somehow she unglued her tongue from the roof of her mouth, but her attempt at a reply was hopelessly incoherent.

"I thought . . . you said . . . you gave me the impression that you'd never come back here."

The amusement in his eyes was swallowed up into a flat darkness that repelled any attempt to read his thoughts. "I'm here. That doesn't mean I'm back," he stated equivocally.

"Then why come?" she asked, her heart leaping with the wild hope that he had actually spoken the reverse truth, and it was *he* who had been unable to keep away from *her*.

He shrugged. "For this particular job, well, I'm more familiar with the habits of whales than most people are, and I know the waters of this bay like the back of my hand. For today I've taken over from the regular captain. You want a smooth operation with your Japanese tourists. I promised you that, and when I promise something I deliver."

Unfortunately, the explanation sounded all too reasonable. Tiffany felt a deep stab of disappointment. Of course, the scenario that had leaped into her mind was wild and improbable, but she still wished that Joel had come for personal reasons and not for practical ones. Before she could recover herself, he had shifted his attention to Alan, his face softening into a friendly smile.

"Your aunt is a bit slow in introducing us. I'm Joel Faber, Alan."

"Alan Tay James," came the prompt response. Alan's expressive face beamed with delight as he stepped forward to shake the hand Joel offered him. "Thanks for coming, Mr Faber. I was scared stiff that Aunt Tiff had made a big mistake until you came through with the goods."

"Just between you and me, she did, Alan. Next time you get a call like that, the thing to do is say you'll ring back and confirm. Then make sure you can deliver before you take the booking. Get yourself a list of charter contacts."

"I've got that done now," Alan told him eagerly. "I won't get flustered again, Mr. Faber."

"OK," Joel approved. "I guess we both have to remember that your aunt is a very enterprising lady. I admire her nerve, but you won't always have her at your side, Alan.'' He gave the boy a man-to-man grin. ''On the other hand, if anyone's learned to stand up for himself, I figure it's you.''

Alan laughed in pride and pleasure at Joel's compliment. ''Thanks, Mr Faber. I typed up this schedule for you. I hope it's OK.''

Joel glanced over the sheet Alan handed him. ''I'm sure we can keep to that. No worries, Alan. Just send the passengers on board, take their money and leave the rest to me.''

''I'll do that! Thanks again, Mr Faber. It was a pleasure meeting you. And I think your yacht's fantastic!''

''Thanks, Alan.''

They shook hands in a spirit of mutual respect. From the look on Alan's face when he turned around, Tiffany guessed he had found another hero to worship. She couldn't help feeling immensely gratified by the way Joel had handled her nephew. There had not been the slightest patronage in any of his words or manner. Nothing false or forced. In fact, she well understood Alan's response to him. Joel Faber had been just like Zachary Lee in his

treatment of the boy, a subtle acknow-
ledgement of his courage, appreciation of his
abilities and total acceptance of him as a
fellow human being.

"Coming, Aunt Tiff?" Alan prompted.

"In a minute, Alan. Go on ahead. I want
a quick word with Mr Faber."

Joel raised a mockingly quizzical eyebrow
at her as soon as Alan left them alone. If it
was supposed to suggest he had just put on a
performance, Tiffany didn't believe it.
Whatever he had been over the past twenty
years, whatever he was now, the inner core of
the man was good. And the attraction she felt
toward him had just increased a hundredfold.

"You keep saying it's too late. But it's not,"
she said quietly, her eyes challenging his with
intense conviction.

His mouth curled in irony. "I remember
being fifteen. It was a long time ago, Tiffany.
A couple of lifetimes ago."

She shook her head, knowing instinctively
that he was hiding things, either from her,
from himself or from both of them. What he
had shown Alan was the real Joel Faber. She
was certain of it.

"This isn't business...what you're doing today," she said slowly. "We could have put a local pilot in beside your captain. You didn't have to come, Joel." She smiled at him and said something he must have heard at least once before in his life, either from his mother or grandmother. "Shame the devil," she soothed, "and tell the truth."

He stared at her for several seconds, and again she felt that deep hunger reaching out to her. It made her whole body tingle with a kind of electric expectancy. The stretch jeans she wore suddenly felt too clinging and hot. She was conscious of her breasts thrusting against the soft cotton T-shirt, her nipples hardening into taut peaks. Her heart seemed to beat loudly in her ears. Even when he wrenched those darkly devouring eyes away and turned his head to scan the waters of the bay, the tension between them didn't lessen. She knew intuitively that he was as intensely aware of her as she was of him.

"Perhaps I wanted to see the whales again," he said in his enigmatic way.

Tiffany heaved a disappointed sigh. "I'm glad you'll find some pleasure in the day, then," she said flatly. "I hated to think that *you* were hating it. Having come here."

He had set himself apart from her—apart from everyone—and suddenly she couldn't bear it. She walked up to him, planted her hands on his rigid shoulders and pressed a light kiss on his cheek. "Thanks for making Alan's day, Joel," she said huskily.

"Make mine!" he rasped, and caught her to him with iron-tight arms.

His head swooped down to hers. He didn't even meet her eyes. He kissed her blindly, with so much pent-up need and passion that Tiffany was swept into a maelstrom of sensation that shattered any faculty for reaction. Or decision-making. His mouth plundered hers, insisting on a response that she blindly gave, making an instinctive attack on the inner man that he had denied to her and himself. The need to fight past his reticence, to break down his defenses, to know him as she wanted to know him, drowned out every other consideration. His hands dragged down her body, pressing, moulding, imprinting every line and curve of it on his with such intensity that it seemed he sought to absorb the very essence of her into his flesh and bones. Tiffany felt she knew everything about him, every muscle configuration of his body, his strength, warmth, the clean male scent of him, the taste of him; yet still she knew nothing . . . except the intense depth of the insatiable hunger that demanded so much of her.

She gave because she wanted to give, caught up in wave after wave of excitement that was both addictive and compelling. She would have given him everything then and there if they had been in a more private place. Her whole body yearned to join with his, and a moan of sheer animal wanting tore from her throat as he dug his fingers around her buttocks and rolled her around the throbbing hardness of his arousal. Her breasts quivered with sensitivity against the quick expansion of his chest. His lips broke away from hers and found other urgent things to do around her face, her eyes, her ears. He sucked in a deep steadying breath.

"You want me. And God knows I want you. More than I've wanted most anything else in my life," he whispered hoarsely. "The favours are done. This is just us, Tiffany.

Because we want to So let it be. You want this as much as I do."

She opened her eyes. His were a dark blaze of desire that was ready to consume every part of her, right down to the last powdery ashes of all that she was. And what would be left then? Anything? Or a bleak emptiness from which no life could be drawn? She didn't know. She could barely think. But she couldn't deny that she wanted him. Her body was screaming out for the physical intimacy he was pressing on her.

Her arms were still around his neck, her body still plastered to his, aware of his need, aware of her own . . . and never had it been so compelling, not with Armand or any other man. It was so right. And yet . . .

"Don't deny me!" he commanded harshly, impatient with her silence. "You're not that petty."

"I won't," she admitted on a ragged sigh.

"Now?" he pressed. "We'll go down to my stateroom."

Was that all he wanted of her? Her body? "No!" The sharp negative flew off her lips.

"Tiffany..." His voice rasped over her quivering nerve ends. His hands pressed an erotic reminder of the urgency of their need.

"Not now!" she cried, her mind and heart attacked by so many uncertainties that she couldn't blindly follow the cravings of her body and forget everything else.

Excited shouts broke into the taut intimacy of the moment. Horns started honking outside. The buses were arriving.

A groan tore from Joel's throat. "You're right," he breathed. "This is not something I want to hurry." His eyes burned down into hers, his inner tension winding around her, binding her to him. "Stay here with me today."

Tiffany hadn't intended staying on the yacht, but then she hadn't known that Joel would be here, and she wasn't really needed elsewhere. "If that's what you want," she conceded. It would give her more time with him, to assess what to do, how best to do it.

"You're what I want," he asserted grimly. "That's what I came for. And that's the truth. But I'm not sure that the devil is shamed by it, Tiffany James."

He loosened his hold on her, lifted a hand to her face and softly stroked a line from temple to chin. The blaze in his eyes dropped to a more gentle simmer. "Maybe you will shame him. If anyone can," he murmured, and there was a touching note of tenderness in his voice.

It hurt to move away from him. The situation, however, left them no choice but to get about their business. Tiffany was torn through with unfulfilled needs, physical, mental and emotional. Her sexual arousal was a long time subsiding, and Joel only had to look at her to remind her of it, to stir flames from the embers. It was intensely disturbing because he kept so much hidden from her in every other sense.

Tiffany did not enjoy the day with Joel Faber, although she knew she should. She was treated to every luxury the yacht had to offer. Every whim or want was granted. She was served with fine wines and the kind of food one only experienced in top restaurants. She mixed with the Japanese businessmen and wives who were their guests. The whales of Haven Bay were an enormous success with them. Miles of film went through cameras and videos. Tiffany hoped that some of it had been bought in the village.

Nothing went wrong. Everything couldn't have been more perfect. But behind it all was the throbbing, pulsing hunger of Joel Faber, and neither his charm of manner nor his knowledgeable conversation on any subject broached defrayed Tiffany's consciousness of that hunger.

It was both exciting and frightening, tempting and repelling. Tiffany told herself she would be mad not to experience what he was offering. He affected her in a way that no other man had even approached—and maybe it would all work out better than her wildest dreams. He would let her in to his innermost secrets, share whatever it was that tortured his dark spirit, share what he had never shared before, forget the past and embrace the kind of future that would bring them both unimaginable happiness.

Then she told herself she was mad to think that she could make any difference to him at all. He was used to having any woman he wanted. He wanted her all the more because she had denied him up until this point. When it was over she would be just another woman he had had, perhaps more satisfying because he had been forced to wait, but the need for her would pass once his appetite was sated. The only thing she could be sure of was that when he started to sate that appetite of his he would take a long time doing it.

And yet, under all her confusion and turbulence of spirit was the sense that they had been meant to come together, that there was purpose in the crossing of their lives. Tiffany didn't know what that purpose was, but somehow a mere sexual connection didn't mean enough. It didn't satisfy her. But if she refused him would he walk away from her again? And never come back? Many men had done that to women before.

The decision weighed heavily on her. When they drew into the wharf at the end of the last trip, the sun was already tipping down behind the dark violet-blue of the Great Dividing Range. Tiffany saw all the passengers off. There was nothing more to do. She knew Joel was expecting her to return to his side, and she was certainly not going to evade the issue between them, but she still wasn't ready to resolve it.

She wandered up to the rear deck and leaned against the railing, where he had been that first night when he had invited her on to the yacht. The sheer coincidence that he had seen the trawler come in, had watched out for her . . . Was it accident or fate? Was there a decision to make now, or would it make itself?

She heard his footsteps but didn't turn around. He leaned against the railing beside her, facing away from the village he hated. She felt his eyes scrutinising her profile, intently probing for her thoughts. His formidable will and presence pressed against her own.

"Tonight, Tiffany. We'll make it ours. Come back with me to Leisure Island. Stay with me." He spoke in a low voice that throbbed into her heart, making it pound in fearful agitation.

"Not tonight, Joel," she answered in a bare little whisper.

There was a long pregnant pause before he pressed again, with a question this time. "Isn't it what you want, Tiffany?"

She turned to him, her eyes searching his for some kind of reassurance. "Perhaps.

You're not the only one who has to search for answers, Joel."

He didn't try to evade what she meant. The hunger was still there as strong as ever. Mixed with it was a raw uncertainty that made him look vulnerable. "I don't know what questions you're asking, let alone the answers you need." His words had a rough edge as though they scraped through emotions that grated against one another. "Whatever it is you want, I'll try and give it to you. If I can. If it's within my...reach."

Was love within his reach? Tiffany wondered. Could she satisfy his needs, whatever they were? And even if she did, would he really try to satisfy hers once he had what he wanted?

He pressed on, softening his voice, using it as compellingly and as seductively as any physical caress. "More than any woman I've ever met, you make me conscious of things I've wanted and never had. And that money can't buy. But I can't tell you where this path leads, Tiffany. I won't lie to you about that. I simply don't know. I only know that if I don't have you I'll always wonder what I missed."

"Yes," she murmured. She understood that. And she appreciated his honesty. "I won't lie to you either, Joel. Something about you draws me to you very strongly. As silly as it sounds, I almost feel...protective. I'm afraid that something that could be very special might be destroyed if I...do the wrong thing."

"How can it be wrong?" he dismissed impatiently. "I know intuitively that it is right. I've never felt anything more right." His eyes stabbed home the point as he added, "And you were with me all the way this morning, Tiffany. You wanted me then. You still do. Don't confuse yourself over what's self-evident!"

"It's not that simple, Joel," she argued, her voice gathering passion as she put her uncertainties into words. "I feel that you won't really let me into your life. You've erected barriers that you won't let me cross. Anyone cross. I don't want to make love with you...and feel alone afterwards." Tears welled into her eyes. "I'm sorry. I can't go with you. I won't do it."

Even through the film of tears she could see his need raging against her fears. "It might be different with you," he rasped. "If it can be with anyone it would be with you, Tiffany." He picked up her hand, interlaced his fingers with hers and gripped hard. "Take a chance...*this* chance...with me."

She felt a dark despair behind his words and almost caved in. The urge to give him all he wanted from her clawed through her heart. But her mind argued that the giving would be all one way. She could not avoid being conscious that for him it was only a trial for something possible and in no way a commitment towards either her or the future.

Sadly, regretfully, she shook her head. "It won't work, Joel. Not the way things are."

Frustration tightened his face and an angry bitterness flashed from his eyes. "Perhaps I should have told you a pack of lies."

"I'd have known, Joel," she cut in sharply. "Don't belittle my intelligence."

His eyes warred fiercely with hers, then retreated into grim mockery. He released her hand, making a dismissive little gesture that denied any force on his part. His voice was a light cutting edge that sliced under her skin, making her painfully aware of his displeasure.

"So where do we go from here? I want you so damn much I'm not sleeping nights for thinking of what it might be like. And I'm not going to walk away from it now, Tiffany. One day soon we're going to be together, whatever the hell you think. And wherever the hell it leads. I don't care. You are going to take that journey with me because I won't give up until you give in."

Relief washed through her. It wasn't the end. She tested him with a tentative smile. "Then I guess I'll see you at Q2RV to-morrow. If you're there. If you want to be there."

His mouth took on a sardonic curl. "It would save me sending a car for you if you came home with me tonight. Then I could personally escort you."

"I'll make my own way," she said firmly.

He heaved a sigh that was full of frustrated resignation. "I'll send the car."

"You don't have to."

"I'm a stickler for detail," he said drily. "I like performance. The car will call for you, as arranged, at eight o'clock."

His eyes glittered with challenging deter-mination as he added, "I'll be there at Q2RV to lend authority to your new position. I won't stay. That would give the game away. And if nothing else, I've learned patience in getting the things I want. Sooner or later, you and I are going to come to terms, Tiffany James. The sooner, the better. But I'm prepared to wait. And when we do, it won't have a damned thing to do with Haven Bay or Nerida Bellamy or anything else. All it will have to do with is you and me.''

She gave him a shaky smile. ''I guess I'd like that. The right company at the right time.''

His laugh was short, sharp and mocking. ''There's nothing rational about this, Tiffany. I gave up on rationality days ago. Fight it if you like. I've stopped. The next move is up to you. But whatever you do, I'll win.''

''For your sake, I hope so. But what do you want to win, Joel? Ask yourself that,'' she said, her eyes challenging his as she gave his hand a quick press. Then before he could make any verbal or physical response, she swung away and moved swiftly to the gangway that took her to the wharf and back to the safety of Haven Bay.

She didn't glance back. When she reached the old stone wall that ringed the harbour and put her out of easy sight from the yacht, she turned. Joel hadn't watched her leave. He was no longer at the railing. He was nowhere to be seen. She had returned to the village he hated, and even before the mooring ropes had been untied, the engines of *Liberty* had started up ready to take him away, back to his fortress home on Leisure Island.

Tiffany leaned her elbows on the wall and watched the yacht draw away. The sense of loss and frustration was a physical ache inside her, but there was no feeling of emptiness. Anticipation bubbled through her mind. Tomorrow, she thought, was another day.... There had to be some way to reach into the heart and mind of Joel Faber. Tiffany resolved to find it.

# CHAPTER NINE

As PROMISED, the car arrived for Tiffany at eight o'clock on Monday morning. It was a kind of car that had never before been seen in Haven Bay. Despite the recent horde of tourists, no one yet had toured around in a stately limousine. And this car was not even stately or discreet. The long, high-bodied and totally luxurious Bentley was bright red. As a status symbol it was the ultimate traffic stopper!

It looked hopelessly incongruous parked outside Carol's modest weatherboard cottage in the modest little street. Curtains twitched up and down the rows of houses. Children raced to examine this fabulous curiosity. Alan was first and foremost among them, positively goggling at the splendor of Aunt Tiff's transport.

The upholstery was cream leather outlined with red piping. Everything gleamed, including the uniformed chauffeur, who climbed out of the driver's seat and stood at attention by the passenger door. He good-naturedly answered the children's questions while he waited for Tiffany to descend upon him.

Carol had accompanied Tiffany out to the veranda. There they both automatically paused, staggered by the sheer extravagance of what had been provided. The same question went through both their minds. Was such a car supplied to other managing directors of television stations?

"I think there is more to this than you have told me, Tiffany," Carol concluded, slanting her knowing dark eyes up at her taller sister. "Joel Faber must think a lot of you."

"It must go with the job," Tiffany concluded out loud, but her mind was very active on the subject. A Bentley, of all cars! She wondered if Joel Faber had remembered her claim of coming to his yacht party in one. On the other hand, it might be a not so subtle hint of what he could give her if she chose to give in to him. If this was bribery, he was certainly doing it on an enormous scale!

Tiffany squared her shoulders. No way was she going to be bought. By anyone. Armand had tried that. It didn't work with her.

However, she instantly decided she had better buy herself some executive-type clothes to go with the car. Her blue summer suit would pass muster today. On the whole, though, her wardrobe consisted mainly of casual tourist-type clothes that were not at all suitable for the image Joel Faber obviously wanted her to project. If this was all for Nerida's benefit, which was a possibility that could not be dismissed, she owed Joel her full co-operation.

She kissed Carol goodbye and sailed down the front path, a decided lilt of anticipation in her step. "Daring" and "style", she thought, smiling to herself. "A very enterprising lady." She might very well give the ratings at Q2RV, and Joel Faber, a jolly good shake! This car was not about to intimidate or influence her. If it was her right to use it, then use it she would, as though she took it all for granted.

"Good morning, Miss James," the chauffeur intoned and swept the door open for her to step inside.

Tiffany paused, smiling up at the man in sheer high spirits. "Good morning to you, too, sir. May I ask you your name?"

"Payton, miss," he said, completely poker-faced.

She laughed. Joel *had* remembered. A stickler for detail, he had said, and she could not help but be amused by this detail. "That can't be your real name," she said with utter certainty. "It isn't, is it?"

His poker face cracked into a conspiratorial little smile. "No, miss. But it's my name for this job. Mr Faber's orders. If anyone asks, I'm Payton. Mr Faber said you'd understand, miss."

"Of course. Thank you, Payton."

She was starting to get on to Joel Faber's wavelength. When he set out to play a game, he played it to the hilt. And he liked performance. Tiffany liked performance, too. This new job was going to be very interesting.

She climbed in and sank into more luxurious comfort than she had ever experienced in any car before. The chauffeur closed her door and resettled himself in the driver's seat. As the powerful turbo engine purred into life, she grinned and waved at Alan, who was directing the children to stand back out of the way. He grinned and waved back. Tiffany suspected that his respect for Joel Faber had risen several more notches. It was an unfortunate fact of life that status symbols had this effect on young people.

She hoped once again that the residents of Haven Bay would not falter over their newfound tourist industry, but she had done all she could for the time being. She nursed a hope that Joel might yet be persuaded to throw his weight behind it. But if not, someone else surely would if things kept going as well as they had started.

As the gleaming red Bentley left the village behind, Tiffany had the sense of embarking on a new and far more personal adventure. Of course she would keep an eye on what was happening in Haven Bay during the next month. Carol and Alan would keep her posted with reports. But today was the first real start of developing a relationship with Joel Faber, and that was of paramount interest to her.

Her chauffeur delivered her right to the door of Q2RV's administration wing. ''Just call Reception when you want the car, Miss James, and I'll have it here waiting for you,'' he told her respectfully as he held open the passenger door for Tiffany to alight.

She smiled up at him, grateful for his advice on how she was supposed to act. She had noted the empty parking space assigned to the managing director as they passed it, but apparently she was not expected to walk even a short distance.

"Thank you, Payton," she said warmly. "I hope you have as good a day as I intend to have."

A marvellous ebullience was running through her brain. It took considerable control to maintain poise and dignity as she stepped inside Q2RV's main reception area. She was, of course, known by sight because of the documentary. A man instantly rose from a chair to greet her and offer himself as escort to the boardroom, where Joel Faber and all the heads of departments were waiting for her.

Tiffany didn't chat to him as they walked through the corridors. Nor did she meet the furtive looks thrown at her by passersby. She intended to cement her position first. Then she would sort out whatever she needed to sort out among the workers here. She gave every appearance of moving with authority, but her stomach was fluttering with nervous antici-

pation. Apparently Joel had decided not to
have any private meeting with her this
morning, which made the situation rather
tricky. But Tiffany was not deterred from her
purpose.

The boardroom seemed full of men, and
they all rose from their chairs when Tiffany
entered. Joel Faber came forward to greet her,
moving from the head of the table with an
unhurried air, as if nothing the least bit unusual was happening. The cut of his three-
piece grey suit automatically placed him at the
top of any corporate ladder, but, clothing
apart, he had the kind of presence that would
have dominated any group. A lone wolf. One
that everyone skirted with intense wariness.

He was smooth—very smooth—projecting
just the right amount of polite respect. "Miss
James..." His hand curled around hers,
warm, strong and lingeringly possessive. In
sharp contrast his eyes were coolly self-
possessed, giving away nothing of his
thoughts or feelings. But his lips twitched a
little as he asked, "I trust your trip in
was... satisfactory."

"Payton, as you know, is very reliable," she
tossed back drily, hoping that the mad accel-

eration of her pulse rate was successfully hidden.

He had a bit of trouble controlling his mouth. A slight twitch kept teasing his lips. "It's becoming increasingly rare to find anyone reliable these days," he remarked, a meaning gleam sneaking into his eyes. "Consistency is one of the qualities I value."

"Not when it's attached to something that's wrong. Like the ratings here at Q2RV."

It pulled him up and turned him serious. "Of course," he agreed, and released her hand to take a light grasp on her elbow. "Let's get straight to business."

He steered her to the chair to the immediate right of his position at the head of the table. He saw her seated, gestured for everyone else to sit down, then addressed the assemblage with brisk efficiency.

"Miss James, as you all know, is taking over the position of managing director as of now. I expect you all to give her every co-operation in supplying whatever information she requires, and in following any directives she chooses to give you. The ratings, as you are well aware, leave much to be desired. I will not waste time with introductions now. Those of you who have not met Miss James can make yourselves known to her after this meeting. I trust you will pull together as a team to achieve what we all want."

He turned to Tiffany with an encouraging half smile. "Now I'm sure Miss James would like to say a few words to you. Miss James?"

"Thank you, Mr Faber."

He sat down as Tiffany rose to her feet. She was pleased to see that there were two women seated near the other end of the table. It helped to make her feel less isolated in this predominantly male group. She needed every bit of confidence she could glean for what she was about to say. She did not think Joel Faber was going to look quite so relaxed and complacent once she was into the speech she intended to make.

The eyes focused on her from around the table were wary. Tiffany knew from experience that people resisted change. It unsettled them, worried them, rattled their sense of complacency and gave them feelings of insecurity. What she had to do was inspire them with the hope for something better, persuade them to be more flexible in their thinking.

She bestowed a friendly smile on everyone. It was important to invite them on to the team that she would lead to more successful future ratings, if the Fates were kind. But she also needed their co-operation and their loyalty. Nothing ventured, nothing gained, she recited to herself, and took the dive she had planned.

" 'This day is called the feast of Crispin,' " she quoted without preamble. "St Crispin's Day," she added for good measure.

It won attention. Blank incomprehension stared at her from every face.

"Nearly six hundred years ago, the historic battle of Agincourt was fought on St Crispin's day," Tiffany enlightened them in a matter-of-fact tone, then plunged into the meat of her speech.

"It is no exaggeration to say that Q2RV is in the same embattled situation as the beleaguered English were against the might of the French army on the plains of Agincourt. The odds for coming out on top were not good. And the fight to do so required courage, fortitude and the absolute conviction that any other course of action was unacceptable."

There was a flicker of interest now.

Tiffany took a quick breath. "So I will make the same offer to you as King Henry V made to his troops. If you have no stomach for the fight ahead of us, if you prefer to leave now, do so. The really hard decision to make is to remain. Because I promise you only blood, sweat and tears, and plenty of them. I will always be available to you, twenty-four hours a day, but until the ratings are re-established at a favourable level, I will expect the same effort from all of you. So please...those of you who prefer to take other options open to them, leave now. With what is coming, there is no disgrace in going."

She had their attention completely. No one moved. Not an eyelid blinked. They didn't even glance at Joel Faber to see what he was thinking. Neither did Tiffany. At this point she couldn't afford to. She let a tense moment pass. No one got up to go.

She smiled to relieve the tension. "I also believe that all the glory will be in staying. However, it will not be easy. Let me say at the outset that what we have here at Q2RV is a problem than cannot be fixed with a patch-up job. That's been tried. It's failed. Time and time again. What we need is a full frontal attack. Revolutionary ideas. I'm going to start off by giving you a brief outline of my plan to boost the ratings. Then I want you to—''

''Will you please hold it there for a moment, Miss James?'' Joel Faber's voice cut in, an incised edge of steel.

This was the crunch, Tiffany thought, her heart squeezing tight. Somehow she kept a completely bland expression on her face as she turned to him. It was obvious to her that he was barely holding himself in check. His face was a tight mask. There was a glitter in his eyes that promised danger and the firing line was straight at her.

''You wish to make some comment, Mr Faber?'' she asked in a calm enquiring lilt. Adrenalin was pumping through her at a dizzying rate.

He pushed up from his chair, emanating aggressive purpose from every inch of his formidable height. ''Your plan—'' He seemed to choke on the word. ''May I have a moment with you? In private.''

''Of course, Mr Faber,'' she said with far more aplomb than she felt. She understood he was about to tear her to pieces for daring to go above what he had laid down. But no way was she going to recant!

She flashed a smile around the table. "Please excuse me. I'll be back shortly." Maybe she would, maybe she wouldn't, but she would carry the flag until she was definitely dropped!

Joel Faber led the way to the door and held it open for Tiffany. She paused before making her exit, her eyes sweeping the faces that had all turned to watch them go. Her chin lifted a little with undaunted authority.

"Mr Faber is quite right," she said, determined that they shouldn't be left with any loss of confidence in her position. "This intermission will give you all time to examine your consciences. Talk to one another if you choose, and make the future commitment that is necessary if we're going to get this business up and running."

She heard Joel Faber's sharp intake of breath and swept past him with no more ado. Once out in the corridor, he took her arm in an iron grasp and steered her to an unoccupied office that had all the executive trappings that the chauffeured Bentley had led her to expect for her elevated position.

Tiffany denied the sickening churn in her stomach and brightly asked, "Is this my office?"

"It was to be," Joel growled, swinging her around to face him, his fingers digging hard into the soft flesh of her upper arms. "What the hell are you playing at, Tiffany?" he seethed at her. "You know damned well this is a *nominal* position! And you agreed to that!"

"Yes, I did. I've had to change my mind. And rightly so. Because—"

"Do you backtrack on everything you say?" he demanded, his eyes flaring with bitter accusation.

"Never! I carry through to the bitter end. As you will see if—"

"Were you playing with me yesterday?"

"I've never played with another human being in my life!" she defended hotly, appalled that he should think so.

His mouth curled in savage irony. "No. You only tied me in knots and walked away. And now you're twisting and changing things again."

"This is very simple and straightforward, Joel," she appealed quickly.

"Nothing with you is simple and straight-forward!" he grated. "Nothing!"

He released her arms with vehement passion, throwing out his own hands in a gesture of deep exasperation and slicing the air with them. He paced across the room, emanating a violence of feeling that he was having difficulty in bringing under control. Yet the determined set of his shoulders indicated he would not let it get the better of him.

Tiffany held her tongue, shaken by Joel's angry outburst, but oddly gratified by his loss of composure. Anything was better than the cynical mask he usually hid behind. Maybe she had reached him in a way she hadn't even imagined, forcing him to rethink things he had taken for granted over the years.

When he swung around it was with a belligerent glare. "You agreed to a nominal position, Tiffany," he reminded her again, challenging her to deny it. "What are you doing to me?"

She took a deep breath and tried to inject calm reason into her voice. "Joel, you're going to fire me. That's your plan. You *accepted* failure without even trying. I can't do that. I have to put my best foot forward, try as hard as I can. I know no other way. This *cynical* scheme of yours would destroy us. It would destroy my belief in myself. I'm sorry. But I can't live by your values."

"And I can't live by yours," he snapped. "You've changed our agreement——"

"You forced it on me."

"And rightly so!"

"No!" She tried again, desperate to make him understand. "Joel, you said I had to be here for a month. Since I have to be here, and you're going to sell anyway, I have to have a go at——"

"No! No. No. No! We stick to the agreement."

"Why?" she demanded, her own belligerence surging to the fore. "You can't really expect me to sit here for a month like an idle dummy, twiddling my thumbs, looking at fools and foolishness. It's simply not viable. We'll both look like simpletons, you for hiring me, and me for being hopelessly ineffective."

"I'll wear it," he rasped. "If I have to."

Tiffany's chin jerked up in defiance. "Well, I won't!"

His mouth thinned. "I am not about to renegotiate the situation, Tiffany."

"Then fire me now! I'm not going to wait around here for a month, doing nothing, just for you to fire me at the end of it. If you want to deny me any chance of doing something constructive, let's get rid of it all now, Joel. You can announce that we've had an irreconcilable difference of opinion. It'll cost you a lot less than paying for a monthlong charade."

"And you get to walk away from me again," he mocked.

The heated flush in her cheeks ebbed away. "That's up to you, Joel," she said with quiet dignity. "It takes two people to make an agreement. Force is a poor bedfellow."

A bleak look sharpened the angles of his face. He turned away and walked over to the window behind the huge executive desk. He stood there staring out, his back rigidly turned to her as if denying that she meant anything to him.

Tiffany had an awful hollow feeling that he was completely intractable, that she was about to lose him. The silence in the room grew more and more oppressive. The distant sound of a carillon of bells from some nearby church tower made her feel even worse. It seemed as though the bells were tolling the end of all her hopes. The echo of them was still in her ears when Joel swung his attention back to her. He only half turned, and he gave her that weighing look that made her feel he was tensed to retreat at any signal that he interpreted as hostile.

"You won't accept anything else, will you?"

It was more a flat statement than a question. Tiffany wasn't sure how much he was covering with those words. She was sorely tempted to say she would accept anything at all. The thought of not having any more to do with him in the future had her stomach in knots. Yet what good could it be if she didn't stay true to herself?

"I've never been a cipher. The cap simply doesn't fit, Joel," she said, half-pleading. Then her innate pride and sense of self-worth added their strength to her voice. "Fail I might, but I will never be a figurehead for failure. Not ever."

He nodded. But there was still that hard watchful look in his eyes as he slowly walked back to her. Tiffany held her breath, unsure of what was coming next. He reached up and softly cupped her chin, tilting it a little higher. His eyes bored into hers, intent on probing her soul.

"Are your ambitions so all-important, Tiffany? Is your need for success so consuming that—"

"No!" she cried out in anguished protest. "Don't you understand, Joel? I want to do something for you!"

"For me?" he repeated, as if tasting words that were entirely foreign to him. Then in a sudden blaze of deep frustration he dismissed her argument. "You know damned well what I want from you, Tiffany. This is another one of your sleight-of-hand tricks."

"It's not!" Her eyes begged him to understand. "You gave me what I wanted to promote the documentary on Haven Bay. You gave me the yacht when we needed it most. You gave me a protective cover from that dreadful Nerida woman, even though it was probably serving your own interests, too. And now...the Bentley...and all that. I can't do what you ask, Joel. It's not right for me. But I want to do something for you. So, please, let me try, Joel. It's the least I can do, and

I'll give it my best shot. I promise you that. Truly I will.''

His eyes raked hers for several tense moments, then fell to her mouth. His fingers trailed down to the rapid pulse beat at the base of her throat, paused there for one breath taking moment, then dropped away. Tiffany's lips had actually quivered, wanting the kiss that did not come. His gaze lifted to hers again, and unaccountably his eyes looked pained.

''You're playing with high stakes, Tiffany,'' he said quietly. ''And you're taking a lot of people along for the ride. This is not just between you and me.''

She swallowed. Her throat had gone bone-dry. ''It's worth a try, isn't it?''

His mouth quirked into an ironic little smile. ''A lot of things are worth a try. It's just that with you, I'm always coming out at the losing end. And the cost keeps going up.''

It must seem that way to him, Tiffany thought despondently. She wondered if she had gone too far. In her need to reach him, maybe she *had* blinded herself to the consequences of failure.

''You are one very expensive lady, Tiffany James,'' he said drily. ''I hope you appreciate the loss of goodwill if the ratings go down in a screaming heap.''

She stared blankly at him for a moment, deep in self-doubt. Then came the jolt of realisation that he intended to let her go ahead. It instantly refired her natural optimism. ''I'm sure I can get them to rise, Joel,'' she said earnestly. ''And should I run into trouble, I'll ask for help.''

''Zachary Lee?'' He gave a soft little laugh that sent tingles right down her spine. ''You and your family,'' he gently mocked, then started to move away from her towards the door.

''Joel?'' He was leaving her! Without pressing her for anything!

''I've left a month's salary for you on the desk. You have a completely free hand. I won't interfere.'' He paused to look back at her, his hand already on the doorknob. ''Wait here five minutes. I'm going back to the boardroom alone to give them *my* 'blood-upon-the-waters' speech. It's to reinforce your authority, and to tell them to back you or get out. Then I'll leave them to you.''

"Aren't you going to be here with me for the next month?" she asked, confused by his abrupt volte-face on the whole issue, and not wanting him to leave her again. Not, at least, until she had figured out what all this meant.

"It's best if I stay away," he stated flatly. "People will think I'm riding on your shoulders otherwise. It will detract from your authority. And I have other things to do, Tiffany. You want to do something for me? This is my gift to you, no strings attached. If you can do it, do it. And I hope, for both our sakes, that you succeed."

"But..." She lifted her hands helplessly. "If you're not going to be here, how can I reach you?"

His mouth twisted, but not with cynicism, more in self-musing. "You've been reaching me from the first moment we met." He shook his head, then gave her a long searching look. "This time I'll reach you, Tiffany James. When it becomes necessary."

And on that enigmatic note he left her.

Tiffany stared at the closed door, telling herself she should feel jubilant. She had won the battle, hadn't she? She could try out whatever she wanted. A free hand!

Except she didn't feel free at all. And didn't want to be free, either! More than anything else, she wanted Joel Faber to love her so much that he wanted to share everything with her.

A shuddering little sigh whispered from her lips.

She wished he had kissed her again.

Meanwhile she had a television station to run.

She had better start running it.

Tiffany glanced at her watch. Joel had told her to wait five minutes. She paced around the office, vaguely noting how spacious and comfortable it was, as well as functional for her needs. A couple of lush potted plants broke up the neutral colour scheme and some rather impressive paintings dressed the walls.

She opened a door and found that it led to an equally comfortable and functional bedroom with an en suite bathroom. Handy if she needed to stay here twenty-four hours a day, Tiffany thought with approval. Also handy for a seduction, if that had been in Joel's mind when he had her installed here.

She remembered the month's salary he had left behind on the desk. The salary she hadn't been supposed to really earn in her "nominal" position. Tiffany hurried back to the desk, slit the envelope open and extracted a cheque for an amount so staggering that it could only be called immoral under the circumstances that Joel had wanted her to keep to. She doubted that even a top-notch manager with years of proved success behind him would command such a sum. No. The Bentley, the money, the status. They had been the carrots to draw her into Joel's game, to help him win!

She had been so right to change the rules this morning. Not that she could have done anything else and kept any self-respect at all. But by fighting him she had somehow changed the game. Where it now led, she had no idea. Joel was dropping out of her life again and Tiffany wasn't at all sure what that meant. If he had given up on pursuing her in the way he had planned . . . had he decided to simply let her go?

She checked her watch. The five minutes were up. She set off back to the boardroom. Joel was already gone when she re-entered. But he would come back to her, she told herself. If he didn't, she would reach him again. Somehow, sometime, she was going to reach into that dark soul of his and make him see things by a different light. She wasn't about to let him go. Not now. Not ever!

There were no vacant places at the table. Except Joel's. When she smiled at the expectant faces turned to her, the smile was returned this time. It appeared that they were all on the team and ready to gird their loins for the cause. Tiffany did not return to her former chair. She took Joel's position at the head of the table. In this at least, she and he were one.

# CHAPTER TEN

THE FEELING of ebullience didn't last long. The situation at Q2RV was too serious. Joel had been so right when he said this wasn't just between the two of them. She had to succeed for much more than both their sakes. People's jobs and life careers were at stake. Reputations were being laid on the line. There were huge sums of money involved. Old sponsors had to be reassured about programme changes, new sponsors won over. Contracts had to be honoured. Tiffany had to continually fight off the sinking feeling that she had bitten off more than she could possibly chew.

That one-month deadline was her biggest problem. She didn't have the time for a steady long-term campaign. No time for trial and error. Only make-or-break time. She was so busy with meetings and research studies and decision making that she barely had time to brood over what Joel was doing—away from her—and certainly no time to go shopping for clothes.

This latter problem, however, was relatively easy to solve. She summoned the head of the wardrobe department, explained what she wanted, and three of the most exclusive boutiques in Brisbane brought a range of clothes to Tiffany for her selection. The cost of them put a little hole in Joel's cheque, but Tiffany knew the value of a winning image, and the cost was justified when half of her task was inspiring confidence.

The first week was hectic. More times than not Tiffany sent a message to Payton, saying she was staying at Q2RV overnight and would not require the Bentley until the next day. She barely saw Carol and Alan, but they assured her that everything was going fine at Haven Bay.

As a new-look weekly programme was evolved for Q2RV, she had several long telephone conversations with Zachary Lee, seeking his advice on the changes, taking note of his experience and making whatever adjustments he suggested. But for the most part, she listened to her department heads.

Released from the constraint of more orthodox management, they readily voiced criticisms and opened up on ideas that had been nursed privately in case they were scorned or belittled. Tiffany injected her own ideas, quite prepared to have them knocked down. On the whole, however, what was born of these discussions was a kind of hybrid fruit that dared to be original, at least in some aspects. Then she acted, pushing the initiatives that more cautious and conventional management would have hesitated over for a long time. But she didn't have that time. She had to get results on the board.

The second week was the viewer test. The changes made had been advertised and promoted, so it wasn't really a good objective gauge of viewer reaction. Interest had been aroused. Ratings were fair. Some very good. But the acid test would come in the third week when the viewers didn't switch on out of mere curiosity. The high battle tension of the first week had slipped into a mood of cautious optimism by the end of the second.

Tiffany switched attention on to improving the performance of the shows actually produced in the station studios. The news format was given an overhaul with more emphasis on international clips. The afternoon children's show was tightened—more entertainment, less inane chat. Nothing escaped scrutiny, and in some cases programmes were discarded, others revolutionised.

The one show that had consistently earned high ratings was the current affairs programme, which followed the news. This was mainly due to its star, Samantha Redman, whose clear and incisive interviewing technique was much enjoyed by viewers. However, towards the end of the third week disaster struck. Samantha was injured in a car accident on the way in to Q2RV for the nightly show. By the time news of it reached the station, there was no time to find an adequate replacement for her. Gordon West, the executive producer of the show, was tearing his hair out.

''It's the big one! We've been trying for weeks to set up an interview with Neil Patterson, and Samantha was going to crucify that bleeding-heart politician. Give him such a hard time....''

Tiffany understood his frustration all too well. The Neil Patterson interview was a real coup. The man was suspected of misusing millions of dollars from public charities, but somehow he kept flim-flamming the public with his image of caring for the poor and underprivileged. Up until this point he had evaded being pinned down on financial accountability, accusing the media of gutter-sniping. Samantha Redman had intended to rip through his façade. It would have been terrific viewing.

"We've touted this interview in all the newspapers. Everyone's waiting for it," Gordon moaned. "And we won't get that slippery bastard again. Timing's everything!"

"I'll do it." Tiffany's words came out without conscious decision. She was used to doing interviews, although not at this standard. Perhaps she could handle this one. But it would certainly be the most difficult one of her life.

Gordon swallowed Tiffany's decision without a word, but he did look as though he'd taken a double whammy. Such a high-risk gamble was putting both their reputations on the line. But he collected himself, and in the little time there was left, he did his best to drill her on all the background detail.

AT SIX-THIRTY Tiffany was in front of the cameras, introducing Neil Patterson to the viewers. He was a slim, handsome, greying fifty-five, exuding charm and kindly authority. Tiffany instantly put him at ease, enumerating his many fine achievements with charity funds in an admiring tone. She sensed his smugness, knew he thought this interview was going to be a piece of cake. He was an adroit politician used to talking people into believing him. Tiffany was an unknown with a reputation to make. He had every reason to be smug.

He was as smooth as silk and he had a convincing answer for everything. He didn't admit that millions of dollars were missing from the charities he had administered. Records had been lost in a fire. No fault of his. The financial dealings had been so complex no one could remember them. He sounded like a churchwarden.

Tiffany wasn't getting anywhere. She was even beginning to respect Neil Patterson for his prodigious abilities. If this man was guilty of a huge fraud, she wasn't going to prove it. Maybe Samantha Redman might have. Certainly the other woman's aggressive approach would have been more entertaining television than this bland innocuous conversation. The viewers were probably bored to tears. Tiffany's sense of failure was so depressing that it was difficult to focus her mind on asking more and more questions.

Well aware that he was right on top of this interview, Neil Patterson showed his contempt for her by leading the conversation into absolute trivia, even to talking about the huge success he had engineered with charity buttons.

"We put out 3,750,000 last year, sold them through 20,000 outlets, and all but 647 were bought," he crowed delightedly.

"Extraordinary," Tiffany murmured, forcing a sickly smile. "You obviously have an enormous capacity for remembering minute details. You're to be congratulated, Mr. Patterson, on having one of the finest minds I've ever met."

"You flatter me, Miss James," he said with a modest laugh.

"Not at all." Then, barely thinking about it, Tiffany added, "You can remember all this...such precise figures from a relatively small operation a year ago. It's such a shame, when all those millions of charity funds have disappeared, that you can't remember anything at all about those sums of money and where they went."

He looked stunned for a moment, but he swiftly closed the pregnant little silence by plunging into a glib explanation for his selective memory. He was so clever in his defence that Tiffany was slow to realise that she had made a critical point, and then the interview time was up and she didn't get the opportunity to make any capital out of it.

*I've completely fluffed the whole thing,* she berated herself despairingly. Not that it mattered. The viewers probably would have switched off long before Neil Patterson had shown that little inconsistency in his image. She shook her head at Gordon West. He gave her a weak, commiserating smile. They both knew that the show had been a gigantic flop.

As Tiffany retreated to her office to lick her wounds in private, she couldn't help feeling she was just a bungling amateur, plunging around in waters she had no right to be near, let alone trying to captain a ship through them.

She pushed open the office door and faltered to a dead halt when she saw the man by the window. She didn't need to turn on the light to identify him. She would have known that silhouette anywhere. Joel had come. Before the month was up. She didn't want to think about why. She was only conscious of a deep wrenching need for him. She closed the door, stood with her back to it, then almost reluctantly—it felt good just to let his presence seep into her—she snapped on the light switch.

He turned toward her. The tension emanating from him was almost palpable. The dark eyes were full of searing questions.

Tiffany was instantly aware that he knew the disaster she had brought upon herself. Despair swept through her, mixed with a bitter disappointment that it was her failure that had drawn him here, not any desire to be with her.

"Do you know about Samantha Redman's accident?" she asked, struggling to rise above her inner misery.

He nodded. "Only abrasions and concussion, fortunately. But she'll be out for at least a week," he said, subtly pointing out the need for a proper replacement.

"I'm glad she's not badly hurt." Tiffany jerked a hand towards the television set, which had been switched off in her absence from the office. Its blank screen held its own message of defeat, but she asked anyway. "Did you see the show?"

He made a dismissive little gesture. "Most of it."

"Well?" She didn't know why she was pushing it. She knew the answer, and Joel's former reply spelled out his judgement. He had switched off before the end.

"As far as I could see, you didn't bring it off," he stated bluntly, but not unkindly.

She heaved a deep sigh. The truth was the truth, and there was no avoiding it. "I guess I shouldn't have attempted it."

"I gave you complete authority, Tiffany," he said quietly.

Her grimace expressed all the sense of letting him down. "There was no one to take her place. But I should have worked it some other way. If you'd been here..."

"I would have said go ahead."

The words were comforting, although Tiffany didn't stop to analyse why. "So as not to undermine the authority you gave me?"

His mouth curled into an ironic twist. "More likely because of my obsession with you."

"Obsession?"

"For lack of a better word." His eyes gently mocked her questioning. "I want you, Tiffany. I have from the beginning. I don't even care what the price is anymore. Even Q2RV can go by the board.''

One part of Tiffany soared with exultation at this declaration, but the saner part of her mind grasped that he was inadvertently telling her something else, as well. He knew more than she did about what was happening with Q2RV, and it was not good news. Her spirits plunged to a new low. She felt totally wretched about her failure. Even apart from whatever Joel had to tell her, she had undoubtedly lost all credibility as station manager with to-night's fiasco on prime-time television. There could be no climbing out of this situation. She had let everyone down.

Tears welled into her eyes. ''I guess...I'm just not professional enough to handle this job, Joel. And now...after this...'' She lifted her hands in a helpless gesture. ''Why do I always think I can do it?'' The tears over-flowed and spilled down her cheeks.

''Don't cry!'' He moved swiftly towards her. ''It's not worth crying about,'' he said vehemently. ''I wanted you to succeed, Tiffany. I'm sure everyone here wanted you to succeed.''

She looked up at him in watery despair as he pulled her into his arms. ''But I've failed.''

He wrapped her in a cocoon of warmth and strength, gently pressed her head onto his broad shoulder and softly rubbed his cheek over her hair. The words he spoke seemed to come from deep inside him.

"I know what it's like to be blamed for things you've done from the heart. Things that seemed to be in the best interests of those you care about. This is nothing, Tiffany. I've been blamed for other people's deaths. That's something that even time doesn't wash away. I know you wish you could turn back the clock, do it all differently. But what's done is done. And this, it's only a show, Tiffany."

His sympathy ... compassion ... caring ... washed through Tiffany in huge overwhelming waves. He had not come to criticise her or fire her. He had come just to be with her when she needed him most, and she burrowed her face into the curve of his neck and shoulder, loving the feel of him, wanting the taste of him, needing all he could give her.

"Joel," she whispered.

His arms tightened around her, protesting any move away from him. "It's all right," he murmured gruffly. "I only want to hold you. Comfort you."

But she sensed the repressed hunger in him, felt the tautly held control in every tense muscle of his body and knew that he wanted her. As urgently and as compellingly as she wanted him. And maybe the only way she could win his trust was to give in, Tiffany thought in wild justification of surrendering all fight. To give him what he wanted of her. Without reservation. Besides, she had nothing else to gamble with now.

"Joel, I want you to make love to me," she whispered. "Right now. Here and now, Joel."

She felt his chest expand with a swift intake of breath. A hand slid up her back and thrust into her hair, roughly winding through the long tresses and tugging her head back. Doubts tortured the eyes that blazed down at hers.

"Do you really mean that?" he asked, uncertainty straining through the desire that furred his voice.

"Kiss me," she begged him, not wanting any more words, not wanting anything except to lose herself in him.

And she saw the doubts seared away by a flare of hunger. No more words made it past his lips. If there had been any lingering on his tongue, they were lost forever as his mouth met the urgent need of hers in a kiss that clawed at both their souls.

Tiffany didn't want to think, yet hazy thoughts drifted through the compelling waves of sensation that drugged her mind. The more Joel kissed her—and he didn't really stop—the more she seemed to be absorbed into him. She could feel his strength expanding around her, felt herself growing weaker. It didn't worry her. Not for one moment did she hesitate in her surrender. But she was aware that each devouring kiss drew more from her, and as he took what she willingly and recklessly gave him Joel's dominance became more and more powerful.

If he had asked her to walk into the bedroom with him, Tiffany doubted that her legs would have been able to comply. But he didn't ask her. He swept her up in his arms and carried her, his mouth still ravishing hers, relentless in its hunger, mesmerising in its passionate need.

They didn't speak. They were beyond words. Joel undressed her as though she were some exquisite gift to be uncovered with infinite care, caressed with wonder, fondled, worshiped with his hands, with his mouth. There was something more invasive in his sensuality than his passion, hunger giving way to a more enveloping appetite that wanted to taste and feel and scent and know every texture of her being.

Never had Tiffany been touched with such sensitivity, and somehow he made her feel fascinatingly beautiful. Her long hair was the finest, most sensual silk; her throat, shoulders, arms were soft feminine lines that flowed in graceful curves. Her breasts were fashioned to fill his hands, her nipples provocative peaks to be loved by his mouth. Her narrow waist invited his possessive hands. Her rounded hips were womanly beyond compare.

Joel's concentration on her was so total, so consuming, so enthralling that any action from her didn't enter Tiffany's mind. Her whole body seethed with sensations that rendered her incapable of any co-ordinated movement. She quivered to his touch.

Even the short separation while he stripped himself of his own clothes seemed unbearable. She shuddered her relief when he drew her into his arms, gently gathering her in to the vibrant power of his warm nakedness. And when he kissed her this time, his lips cherished hers with a slow seductive dance of sensuality before inviting the deeper intimacy that was so suggestive of the act of love. It was unbelievably erotic with the aggressive maleness of his body rubbing against hers. Desire exploded into an incandescent heat that rampaged through her with devastating force, melting her bones, making her ache with need for him. She was vaguely aware of her nails digging into his skin, clawing his back. Her body arced into his in blindly urgent supplication.

Some inarticulate sound gravelled from his throat, and he moved swiftly to answer her need, lifting her to meet him. She felt him poised against the moist welcoming heat of her body, felt her own muscles convulse in frantic impatience, then with one deep powerful thrust he was inside her, filling her with a wonderful sense of rightness, of relief, of intense riveting pleasure as he reinforced their possession of each other with a rhythm that pushed a storm of sensation through every minute cell in her body. She no longer knew where his body began and hers finished. Her legs wrapped around his in a wild ecstasy of togetherness. Tidal wave followed tidal wave, carrying her to a blissful zenith of exquisite euphoria.

And suddenly it seemed that her senses broke into another more intense dimension. Her whole body pulsed with incredible sensitivity. The musky scents of their bodies intoxicated her. Her eyes clung in fascination to the taut lines of Joel's face, the powerful muscles of his shoulders, the tiny beads of sweat moistening the tight little curls below his throat. Her arms felt limp and heavy, but the desire to touch him was compelling. She lifted her hands and ran the delicate pads of her fingers over his chest, felt the fierce thud of his heart, thrilled to the tremor that contracted his stomach.

He cried out and lost all control, driving her to another incredible level of excitement as he plunged violently to the innermost depths of her and expended himself in a climax that shook them both and pierced her through with the sweetest of pleasures. Her arms were ready to enclose him as he collapsed on top of her, and she hugged his weight to her, exulting in the wonderfully satisfying solidity of their bodies pressed so intimately together. He was part of her, she was part of him, and she didn't want that to end, ever.

He trembled under her touch as she softly slid her hands down his back, reveling in the feel of his muscular strength, the narrowness of his hips, the taut flesh of his buttocks. With a sensuality she hadn't known she possessed she rubbed her legs against his, loving the masculine power of his thighs. Her tongue found the hollow at the base of his throat, explored the salty taste of his skin and thrilled to the vibration of the guttural sound he made as she pressed her lips to the pulse beat she found.

He levered himself up enough to frame her face with his hands, then slowly, lingeringly, trailed soft butterfly kisses around her temples, over each eyelid, down her nose, across her flushed cheeks, and finally seeking the soft sweetness of her mouth—not with hunger but with a tenderness that was almost homage. Then he wrapped her in his arms, cradling her against him as he rolled on to his side. He tucked her head under his chin and began stroking her back, a soft wonderment in every feather-light caress.

For a while Tiffany simply luxuriated in his gentle touch, loving the quiet intimacy of lying together in the peaceful aftermath of passion. She hadn't expected it to be like this with Joel. If anything, she would have expected a wild tempest of lovemaking, quickly over. She was glad it hadn't been that way, yet it disturbed her a little that she had been so passive, so overwhelmed by what he was doing to her. It was as if he hadn't needed her to do anything, or to give him anything except herself.

Joel was a generous lover, just as she had thought he might be the first night they met. Yet the thought of him being like this with other women—all the women who had been in his life before her—made Tiffany shiver with intense distaste.

"Cold?" Joel murmured, brushing his lips over her hair, his warm breath filtering through the thick tresses.

"No," she replied huskily, telling herself that this was different—had to be different—because Joel cared about her. Tiffany knew he did. He couldn't be touching her like this, holding her like this, if he didn't care. It wasn't just an exercise in sensuality. She was certain of it.

But there was one aspect she couldn't dismiss so readily from her mind. Where was this going to lead? She had committed herself, but she knew she had no answering commitment from Joel. Except in this physical sense.

"You realise that I can't let you go now, Tiffany," he said, almost as though he had sensed the uncertainties in her mind. There was a smile of satisfaction in his voice. He rolled her on to her back and leaned over her. He looked happy, and the sharp planes of his face seemed to have lost their edge of hunger. His smile faded as desire furred his voice again. "There's so much more I want of you...."

He kissed her with a slow yearning need that stirred a sense of incompletion deep in her own soul. She knew then they had barely touched the surface of the relationship that could grow between them. Her instincts had not played her false. Perhaps all her life she had subconsciously been waiting for this man, the one designated to be her mate in all things. There was a long way still to go before their understanding of each other was secure, but this was right. The response his body drew from hers was like an awakening that had stunned her with its multitude of sensations. Had he felt the same? she wondered.

"You're beautiful. Beautiful all through," he murmured throatily, his lips moist and arousing as he moved them down her body to reignite her desire for him.

"Joel..." It was both a cry of pleasure and a ragged appeal as his mouth swept gently over her hardened nipple. Her hands curled around his dark head, clutchingly possessive, yet reluctant to halt what was happening. "Joel, there are so many things we have to talk about...." She gasped as his tongue and teeth lovingly caressed the sensitive tip.

"Yes," he murmured, and moved the sweet torment to her other breast.

Tiffany struggled to remember what she had meant to say to him, then gave up the struggle, wanting to make him feel all that he had stirred in her. Above all else she didn't want him to let her go...ever. Her need to keep feeding his need for her swept away all passivity.

Their second coming together was slower, longer but far more intense, as Tiffany made love to Joel with a lack of inhibition that probably would have shocked her if she had once paused to consider it. But she lost herself in the heady pleasure of feeling his firm flesh quiver at her touch, and hearing him groan with the exquisite torture of anticipation driven to its most sensitive heights.

This time she held him entranced while she delighted her own senses, capturing wildly intense responses from him as she caressed his body at will. When he could not bear to wait any longer, she welcomed his fierce need for her, urging him to his climax as she rolled her body in an undulating motion that appeased her own driven desire to take all of him. She changed the pressure on her hips, her stomach, her breasts, one moment thrusting them violently against him, then gracefully and sensuously moving them over his tautly thrusting body, exulting in every shifting contact before driving down to take him deeply inside herself.

Joel quickly caught the mad rhythm of her erotic dance, adding his own exquisitely pleasurable embellishments in between the more savage drumbeat of total penetration. The excitement they built together vibrated through both of them—a single entity—sweeping them to an ecstatic pinnacle of blissful fusion. And at that moment of melting splendour, Tiffany held her hands over Joel's heart, feeling the fierce pulsing of his body beating with hers, and she knew then a contentment she had never known before, a fulfilment she had not thought was possible.

He can't let me go, she thought exultantly. I won't ever let him.

# CHAPTER ELEVEN

RELUCTANTLY TIFFANY dragged her mind off the intimacy of the moment and started turning over the problems that had to be faced. Time had not stood still, and what was going to happen tomorrow couldn't be indefinitely ignored.

Joel, however, seemed to have no inclination to think beyond the present. "You can talk like that to me any time you like," he said, and gave a husky laugh of pleasure. He had never sounded more relaxed. His lips brushed teasingly over hers. "What can I do for you? Tell me, and if it's at all possible, I'll do it."

The deep fervour in his voice curled warmly around Tiffany's heart. "Nothing, Joel." She reached up and stroked his lean cheek. "I don't need you to do anything for me. Because you're beautiful, too."

He turned his face to the palm of her hand, drawing her fingers into his mouth. The suggestiveness of the action made Tiffany's pulse start to race again.

"Joel, there are things we have to decide," she said rather shakily. "Like what I'm going to do about this mess I've got myself into over the current affairs show."

"There's no problem," Joel answered as if it were the simplest thing in the world. "Get someone to fill in until Samantha can make it back. You've got all day tomorrow to set it up. Offer a high enough price and you can buy anyone," he said in that deep cynical vein that Tiffany wished she could eradicate.

It wasn't that simple, anyway. She hadn't forgotten Joel's comment about letting Q2RV go by the board. She didn't want him paying any price for her. Apart from which, her failure affected other people besides herself.

"I can't stay on as managing director," she said decisively. "I've got to resign."

Joel lifted his head, a sharp frown drawing his eyebrows together as he saw the seriousness of her intention. "That isn't necessary, Tiffany," he assured her. "I've seen the preliminary ratings for this week. Some of them are great. In a number of programmes you've obviously struck a responsive chord with viewers that has certainly never been struck before. But a few of the new initiatives haven't worked as well as you probably hoped. Overall, we're doing better."

"How much better?" she demanded eagerly, hoping things weren't as bad as they had seemed.

"A little."

She grimaced. "You mean some of the programmes have bombed out. Like me tonight."

He nodded. "They'll have to be dropped. Or changed. But others have done really well."

"I've failed," she concluded dismally. Joel was obviously trying to put a good face on it for her sake, but hiding her head in the sand was no use at all. "I've failed everyone. You. The sponsors. Myself. The team. The TV station..."

"No," he denied hotly. He placed a silencing finger on her lips as he spoke with persuasive conviction. "We have to be positive and look at what you achieved. We can easily get around the problem areas. What you have succeeded in doing is breaking the stranglehold of managerial mediocrity that Q2RV has been wallowing in. You've shown the road to the future. Concentrate on what has worked. Rework what hasn't."

Tiffany listened, sifting what he was saying against the leaden feeling of defeat. As if sensing she was not completely with him, Joel exerted all his innate magnetism to override any further talk of failure.

"Tiffany, what you've done has far more value than a trivial overall rise in ratings. You've opened up the paths that should be taken. And proved conclusively that some programmes are a dead loss. Your make-or-break policy was the catalyst Q2RV needed to rouse it out of apathy. All that is lacking now is the time to consolidate on the gains you've made. The failures can be totally discarded instead of being allowed to limp along. They can be thrown out and replaced by something with more appeal. You can go on from here. Better than before. That's the end result of what you've done, and that's not failure, Tiffany. That's success."

Looked at from that perspective, the gambles she had taken seemed justified, and Tiffany did not feel quite so bad about her failures. At least she hadn't let Joel down, not in his estimation. "Do you want me to go on?" she asked tentatively, not entirely sure what precisely he did want from her.

The hunger flared in his eyes for a moment, but then subsided into a rueful warmth. "If it's what you want to do, Tiffany, I guess I can keep my distance during the day. As long as you share the nights with me."

Which, to Tiffany at that moment, did not seem a bad idea. Joel kissed her with a rawness of need that expressed all too eloquently what he wanted at night. It left Tiffany wondering if she would ever completely fill the hidden niches of his wants, and lighten all the dark recesses of his soul. It reminded her that there was a lot she didn't know about Joel Faber.

To be attuned to him in every physical sense was basis enough for them to be good lovers together. Tiffany wanted more than that in their relationship, and yet she wasn't certain that there could be more. A man apart, she had characterised him to herself, self-sufficient and seemingly entire unto himself. But she would not accept that he would remain that way. There was something good between them. Something better than he had ever had before. Tiffany had to believe that.

Again she dragged her mind back to the more immediate question of her position at Q2RV. "I appreciate all you say about what's

been achieved, Joel, but I can't stay on here,"
she said decisively.

He frowned. "Because of tonight's show?
It's only one mistake, Tiffany," he argued.

"One mistake too many. I couldn't expect
the staff to give me their trust after that.
They've seen I'm fallible. It's better if you get
a new manager, Joel. Someone who can build
on what we did get right. Who can keep going
forward."

"I'd back you to the hilt, Tiffany."

She shook her head. "You need a proper
professional. Energetic, innovative, daring,
not frightened of making mistakes and big
enough to stride over them. What I did was
amateurish. It's probably all amateurish."

"I'll still back you."

"No, Joel. It's the wrong move."

"You won't change your mind?" he asked,
his eyes assessing her for any sign of wavering.

"It's best this way," she insisted.

He relaxed, his face slowly broadening into
a delighted grin. "I'm glad it's not what you
want. This way, we won't have to be discreet
about anything. Come with me to Leisure
Island, Tiffany. Live with me. There's so
much we can have together."

It was on the tip of her tongue to agree unequivocally. He wasn't offering her marriage,
but the rightness she felt with Joel...the sense
of destiny...her desire to share his life...all
clamored their approval of the arrangement.

Yet some intuitive stirring of unease held
her back. There had been so many curious
reactions from him that she hadn't understood, that had never been explained. She
didn't fully understand the deep inner core of
logic that suggested the question that floated
into her mind, but suddenly it seemed terribly
important for her to know the answer.

"Tell me..." she began, then instinctively
ran her hand down his body in reassurance of
her feeling for him.

"Anything at all," he encouraged with a
smile.

Her eyes focused intensely on his, com-
manding the truth without any evasion at all.
"Tell me who died...who died that you were
blamed for...the night of the storm?"

The smile was swallowed up by an odd
stillness, a stillness that enveloped his whole
body in a kind of frozen rigidity and was
totally impenetrable. He stared back at her
with unflinching directness, but there was

nothing in the darkness of his eyes, nothing but darkness.

A frisson of fear ran down Tiffany's spine. She held her breath, not knowing what to expect, only knowing that she had touched on a place inside him that he had never opened to anyone... and didn't want to open. Yet if he closed her out of that dark secret place...

"Does it matter now?" he asked, his voice utterly toneless, all emotion meticulously strained out of it.

"I can't answer that. You have to tell me," she said, quietly insistent over her own inner turmoil.

She felt his reluctance, sensed the conflict inside him, and when he answered, it seemed each word was coated with poignant pain. "Her name was Mary-Beth Macauley."

Tiffany had desperately wanted him to share this with her, but the recoil that squeezed her heart tight made her wish she hadn't pressed for the knowledge. Yet now that it was given, she couldn't leave it alone.

"She went with you that night on the boat?"

"Yes."

"With your grandfather."

"Yes."

The brevity of his replies made her stretch further. "You loved her, Joel?" she asked, each word a raw scrape through a throat that had gone bone-dry.

"Yes."

No equivocation. No shade of degree. No suggestion that he was too young to love. Just a pure fact. He and Mary-Beth had gone out to face death together, and he had come back alone. And was blamed for it.

Tiffany didn't want to ask the question, but she had to now. She fiercely hoped his answer would clear the dreadful doubt that had risen in her mind, but despair was edging around her heart even as she forced out the words. "Did Mary-Beth...did she have eyes as blue as the blue on a kingfisher?"

His head jerked up in surprise as if he was jolted out of a reminiscence that she had just touched upon with uncanny accuracy. "How did you know that?"

He had obviously forgotten those telling words he had spoken to her that first night, "Damn those eyes! Do you know what you're doing to me?" But Tiffany hadn't forgotten. That was when he had kissed her as though he wanted to drown himself in her, haunted by the memory of the girl he had loved and lost.

His eyes stabbed into hers, hard and suspicious. "Did you get old Garret to tell you all about it?"

"Not really. He never spoke of a girl being involved."

Joel's mouth thinned into a grim line. Bitterness glittered briefly in his eyes. Then, as if he regathered himself from the past and willed all his concentration on to the present, the bitterness receded into a wary watchfulness.

"Does it make any difference to you?" he asked, his voice once again devoid of all emotion.

Mary-Beth was dead. Dead and gone twenty years ago, Tiffany argued desperately to herself, fighting back the tears that pricked at her eyes. Surely Joel had put the memory away once he had decided to pursue her. Mary-Beth was a phantom of the past. Tiffany was the real flesh-and-blood woman in his arms, and she was the woman he wanted to share his life with now.

But for how long, Tiffany didn't know. Joel wasn't promising any permanence. Perhaps it was there, perhaps it wasn't. She had sworn she would never get herself into that kind of no-commitment situation again. And as much as she wanted to be with him—as right as it felt—she could not quite shake off the ghost of Mary-Beth.

"Tiffany?" The slight thread of tension in Joel's voice snapped her attention back to him. She opened her eyes to find him frowning down at her.

"I'm not sure that living together is a good idea," she blurted out. "Not just yet anyway."

The frown deepened. "I'll take care of you, Tiffany. Say whatever you want and I'll give it to you. We'll go anywhere you like. Do whatever takes your fancy...."

"It's not that, Joel," she protested, pained by his predilection for counting on material things to win his way. "I need some time to think about this. Perhaps we both need more time. That Nerida Bellamy is sure to pounce on us, and if it doesn't work out... I don't want to rush into a commitment and then find it's all a mirage that will disappear on me."

"Time." He rolled out the word with heavy irony. "How much time?"

"I'm sorry. I don't know. I just can't come with you tonight, Joel. It's too soon for me," she said raggedly, torn between the desire to stay with him and the urgent need to sort out the past from the present. If there had been no Mary-Beth, no Mary-Beth with eyes the same colour as her own...

"I'm sorry, too. It means I have to wait a bit longer." Then he kissed her with enough passion to forcefully remind her of what they had shared. "Change your mind," he murmured softly, seductively. "State any terms you like."

"No...please," Tiffany replied huskily, wondering if she was being an absolute fool. "Just not...not tonight, Joel."

She couldn't bear to ask him any more about the love he had lost, yet she had to know more. *Garret,* she thought desperately, *I'll ask Garret tomorrow.* Joel had implied that the old fisherman knew. Of course, Garret had to know. It was suddenly clear to Tiffany that all the old-timers at Haven Bay knew. They had blamed Joel for Mary-Beth's death, and that was why Joel hated the place.

The past wasn't dead to Garret, either! It wasn't too long ago to hate. He had encouraged and helped her to get to Joel because of her eyes, using her as a nemesis from the past...to haunt him.

And Joel had said he was obsessed with her.
Not love.
Obsession!
Even with her mind whirling with these re-velations, the temptation to recant and to go with him was still so strong that Tiffany barely forced herself to get up from the bed. She had to keep her eyes averted from Joel to stop herself from weakening as she gathered a change of clothes to take into the bathroom with her. Tomorrow she might be able to think clearly. Tomorrow, after she had forced Garret to tell her everything. She had been under so much pressure with so many things.... It was too much for her tonight.

When she emerged from the bathroom, Joel was fully dressed and seated at the foot of the bed, his arms resting on his knees, his shoulders hunched over, head bent. The forlorn pose and lonely air was instantly shaken off as he stood—straight, tall, tautly composed, once again an indomitable presence in total command of himself, a look of grim determination on his face.

But Tiffany couldn't shake off that poignant image, and her heart went out to him. ''Joel, you've been so good to me. Is there something...anything I can do for you?''

His mouth quirked into a musing little smile. ''Yes. There is.''

Tiffany winced. ''I meant apart from going back to Leisure Island with you.''

''Apart from that,'' he drawled lightly, ''you could get me Zachary Lee.''

She looked at him in bewilderment.

''I need a station manager,'' he reminded her. ''I tried to get him some time ago. He wasn't interested. But if you speak to him, Tiffany, if you make him the offer, he'll listen to you. Tell him he can virtually write his own package deal. I'll back whatever he wants to do, all the way. And if he starts off at Q2RV, and if he's good enough, big enough, we can expand into a network. Even go international. He can head it all, make himself a superstar in the television world if he has the drive to take it on. It's up to him. But the opening is here for him to forge a future that can give him every career satisfaction he wants.''

The generosity of the offer was almost unbelievable, yet Tiffany didn't doubt that Joel meant it. In one bold stroke he had resolved all the problems she had raised at Q2RV. By bringing in her brother, who was a respected professional in the field, Joel would be assuring that no one here would pay any awful price for her failures. Simultaneously, it gave Zachary Lee the opportunity of a lifetime.

The lump of emotion in her throat was too great to circumvent. Tears welled into her eyes as she forced her legs to carry her across the short distance that separated them. She rested her hands against the warm solidity of his chest as she reached up to kiss him.

His hands covered hers, imprisoning them against him. "Tiffany..." It was a hoarse moan of need as her lips left his.

"I just wanted to thank you," she managed shakily.

"No need. It's my gain if I get Zachary Lee," he rasped.

"It's the best present I could give my brother. And you're handing it to me to give it to him," Tiffany corrected him with intense feeling, her love for Zachary Lee mixing with an even stronger emotion that was irrevocably linked to the man who held her to him. "I'll ring Zachary Lee tonight," she promised.

"Do that," Joel said flatly, and slowly drew her hands down to her sides again. He took a card from his shirt pocket and gave it to her. "He can reach me at this number." His eyes met hers with barely restrained hunger. "You can, too, Tiffany. Any time at all."

She nodded, dropping her gaze from his. If he had asked her to go with him once more she would probably have acceded there and then. But he didn't ask. And some thread of common sense dictated that she follow through on what she had decided.

"I'll call you soon," she assured him in a husky whisper. "Goodnight, Joel."

Even as she hurried away from him, she was deeply conscious that this was no parting of the ways. Tonight their lives had become inextricably mingled, and despite any distance that either he or she set up between them there was no going back to an existence where they could ignore each other. Or forget each other. But what kind of future they could forge together was dependent on a lot of things that still had to be determined.

# CHAPTER TWELVE

As SOON AS Payton had the Bentley rolling away from Q2RV, Tiffany used the car telephone to contact Zachary Lee. If her brother accepted Joel's offer, which he surely would, the sooner his change of position could be organised the better. Fortunately, she caught him at home, and in his usual amenable way, Zachary Lee heard her out, carefully weighing all she had told him before speaking his mind.

"Tiff, I don't want you to step down, or step aside. You've got a great future in TV, and it seems to me you're jumping the gun by getting out now," he said, pouring gentle reassurance into his soft melodious voice. "The game is yours for the taking. This show tonight, it's nothing, Sis. Only a one-off. You've made too much of it. You've got a great new career opening out for you. Go for it."

She smiled. It was so typical of Zachary Lee to care about her future ahead of his own. He would never take the job if he thought she was secretly hankering after it.

"I don't want it. I truly don't," she said as emphatically as she could. "Please. Ring Joel. Talk to him. It's the kind of deal that dreams are made of, Zachary Lee. Joel's talking big. In a way that would never be possible for me. I enjoyed doing what I did at Q2RV, but it's not my life, and I never intended it would be. So if you pass up this proposal out of some hopelessly mistaken idea of loyalty to me, I'll be so mad with you...I'll be madder with you than I've ever been in my whole life, and I might never talk to you again."

He laughed, a lovely deep chuckle that always warmed her heart. "Well, I guess I can't afford to let that happen. I'll ring Faber. But Tiff..." All amusement was wiped from his voice, and he spoke with deadly seriousness. "To say the least, you must realise this offer is highly unusual. I've met Joel Faber. This is not his kind of deal. Forgive me for saying it, but he's a man with a purpose. And this time I don't believe his purpose is centred on getting me. I think you'd better tell me what the real position is between you two."

It wasn't exactly an easy position to describe. Tiffany found it difficult to put into words. Zachary Lee didn't seem to care for her hesitation.

"I know it's none of my business, but if you don't tell me, Sis, I'll ask him. If I don't like what he tells me, I might even get angry. I'll probably ask him and get angry anyway, but I'd like to hear your side first."

She heard the low undertone of intense protectiveness behind every word, and sighed. She was old enough to look after herself, and the thought of Zachary Lee getting angry made her smile. It was so incongruous. On the other hand, knowing this gentle brother of hers as well as she did, she was aware that he was quite liable to throw Joel's offer in his face and stuff it in his teeth if he thought Tiffany was being bought or manipulated or seduced by it. And he was certainly big enough and strong enough and forceful enough in his ideas to be extremely capable of doing it.

Joel's cynical words suddenly crossed her mind, "Offer a high enough price and you can buy anyone." Maybe that was what Joel thought he was doing, but Tiffany knew she wasn't being bought.

"Zachary Lee, do you ever wonder how it was that Mum and Dad went to New Orleans just at the particular time they did, so that your life was changed from that point on?'' she asked softly.

There was a slight pause, ''What are you saying, Tiff?''

''I guess I'm saying that there are some things that can't be explained. For better or for worse, they just happen. And I've gone past the point of no return. Nothing you say or do will change it back, Zachary Lee. I want you to take Joel's offer. There aren't any strings attached. Not for you. Not for me. In the end, I'll always do what's right for me.''

If Joel had made the offer with the purpose of keeping some kind of hold on her, it was totally irrelevant anyway. The hold was already too firm to break. It was still a gift as far as Tiffany was concerned, and a gift that Joel wouldn't take back no matter what happened between them. He had proved to her that he was a man of his word, a man of honour who kept his agreements.

''Sis...'' The strained throb in the affectionate term drained into a deep sigh. ''OK, I'll talk it over with him. And he'd better be damned good to you and look after you properly or...or all hell will break loose.''

She ignored his last comment and gave him Joel's number. "Rest easy, Zachary Lee. One thing I have learned is that you can trust Joel Faber to do whatever he promises. You have nothing to worry about," she said firmly, then hung up.

Tiffany had quite a bit to worry about, but just talking to her brother had made some things clearer in her mind. She was not going to let doubts and fears cloud her relationship with Joel. Whatever they had together was better than anything she had had before, and she doubted she would ever feel as much with any other man. Tomorrow she would confront Garret with the name of Mary-Beth Macauley and get the truth of all that had happened on the night of the storm. Then she would know what she was dealing with. Or at least she would have a better idea.

"If you'll pardon me, Miss James—"

Tiffany was startled out of her intense inner reverie by the chauffeur's polite drawing of her attention. Her eyes flew to the rear-vision driving mirror and caught a look of concern on his face.

"I'm sorry, Payton," she rushed out apologetically. "I was so preoccupied with other matters that ... well, I guess you overheard that I've finished up at Q2RV. I don't regret that, but it does mean this is our last trip together, and I want to thank you for having been so patient and kind.''

''It's been a real pleasure working this job, Miss James,'' he said gruffly. ''I just wanted to say, if you'll excuse the liberty, I couldn't help overhearing what you said on the phone about the interview tonight. I guess you've got to see things your way, but the way I see it I reckon you've got it wrong. You led that politician into tripping over his own tongue. It took a while for the penny to drop, to really understand what you did to him. But once the wife and I put it together... My wife thinks it was the smartest thing she's ever seen on TV. And she should know. She watches a lot of it.''

''That's very kind of her. Please tell her... I'm very grateful.'' If there had been a few million more viewers like Mrs Payton, Tiffany reflected, then she really would have been an enormous success.

Payton chuckled in gleeful remembrance. ''I bet Patterson wished he'd swallowed all those charity buttons before he started remembering about them. You sure got him choked on that, Miss James. Stopped him dead. Stands to reason that a guy who can remember everything about little things like buttons has to be lying in his teeth about not remembering big important transactions with millions of dollars. He's done himself in, Miss James. He can talk himself red in the face. No one's going to believe him now.''

A wry little smile curled Tiffany's lips. ''Thanks, Payton, but I don't suppose too many viewers, apart from you and your wife, were still watching by then. It was hardly an entertaining interview.''

''Well, he sort of talked all over you,'' Payton admitted. ''Real full of himself he was, and so slickety-smart it was enough to make you sick. But that's what made it so good when he slipped up blowing his own trumpet. I tell you, Miss James, I've been enjoying it ever since, thinking of that look on his face when he realised he'd convicted himself out of his own mouth. I didn't really pick it up straight away. Neither did the wife.''

Tiffany doubted that many people had. She hadn't picked up on it herself until it was too late.

''But the more I thought about it,'' Payton continued with relish, ''the better it was. In fact, I wish they'd show the whole interview again. Knowing what's coming at the end, it'd make all that guff that came before more..." Payton searched for the right word.

"More pointed?" Tiffany supplied helpfully.

"That's exactly right, Miss James," Payton said with satisfaction. "That's it exactly."

"All that guff" was a fairly exact description of the interview. Tiffany suspected that Payton was being very loyal to her, and wanting to make her feel she had done a better job than she had. She gave him a warm smile. "I wish I'd made more of that point about his memory, but I'm glad you enjoyed it, Payton."

"You just relax now, Miss James," Payton said, flashing her a smile of approval in the mirror. "I'll get you home safe and sound."

"Thank you, Payton. And thank your wife for me."

The number of viewers who had stuck with her to the end of the interview grew to four when Tiffany arrived home to find Carol still up. Her sister insisted that she and Alan thought Tiffany had given Neil Patterson just the right amount of rope to hang himself with.

No one should ever discount the value of family loyalty, Tiffany thought to herself as she finally buried her head in a pillow for the night. It might be biased, but it was comforting.

Carol shook her out of a heavy sleep the next morning. It was barely six o'clock, but Zachary Lee was on the telephone, insisting that he had to speak to her. Tiffany's mind was whirling around some possible conflict between her brother and Joel as she staggered out of bed to take the call.

"What's wrong?" she asked anxiously, forgetting to even say hello.

"How does it feel to be an overnight sensation?"

"What on earth are you talking about?"

"The police have arrested Patterson. He's been formally charged. Hell, they threw the book at him! And that makes you—" Zachary Lee chuckled "—sensational!"

"No!" She couldn't take it in.

"Yes! Last night you put the final nail in any credibility he had left, Tiff. Your interview with him is now the hottest property around."

She was speechless. She felt like the condemned person reprieved from the gallows after the noose had been put around her neck.

"So I thought I'd ring and let you know why I *won't* be getting in touch with Joel Faber," Zachary Lee said meaningly.

*And there goes a promising international career down the drain,* Tiffany thought. "This doesn't change anything!" she protested.

"It changes everything, Tiff! You're on the crest of a great wave. You can ride it to the top."

"I don't want to," she said emphatically. "That was pure luck, Zachary Lee. I'm glad I didn't finish up a failure at Q2RV, but I am finished! And you promised to speak to Joel Faber."

"Don't argue, Tiff. *This* is misplaced family loyalty. Last night's deal is off!"

"It's on! I'm just not interested, Zachary Lee. I've got more important things to do."

"Like what?"

"A bit of living! A bit of loving!"

Silence. Then slowly, "I hope you know what you're doing, Sis."

"If you don't take this job, Zachary Lee, it'll just go begging!"

He sighed. "I'd hate to let it go begging. All right, Tiff. But on one condition."

"Which is?"

"If I ever need advice, I can come to you to get it."

She laughed in relief. "Always, you big silly!"

The smile came back into his voice. "If that's the case, I'm going to ring Joel Faber now."

"And about time, too!"

"And as you know in this business, timing is everything. Don't keep your feet on the ground today, Tiff. Every newshound in this country—including your friend, Nerida—will be after you. Give me time to get things arranged. If I can't make capital out of my sister, then I don't deserve to be in TV. Disappear for the day. When I get in touch with you it will be to do a prime-time, strictly exclusive interview. Can you do that?"

"Sure. It fits in with what I'd planned. I'll persuade Garret to take me out on his trawler. You just leave a message with Alan. He can get us by radio."

"Fine! Let's get moving, little sister!"

The line was abruptly disconnected. Tiffany put down her receiver slowly, wondering if she had just made a bad mistake telling Zachary Lee she was going out on Garret's boat. If he happened to mention to Joel where she was for the day, Joel wasn't going to like it. There was certainly no love lost between him and Garret McKeogh.

But Tiffany was determined now to get to the whole truth of that old tragedy. If Joel didn't like how she did it, she would weather it somehow. If Garret didn't like it, she would point out that he owed it to her. The old man had a lot to answer for, in Tiffany's opinion. And she had better get moving!

When she explained to Alan what was happening, the boy frowned in concern. "I don't think it's a good idea to go out to sea today, Aunt Tiff. The barometer's been falling. Storm warnings are out."

"I'm sure Garret will know when we have to head for home, Alan," Tiffany assured him.

He still didn't like it. "I'll keep in touch on the radio then," he finally conceded.

Unfortunately, Garret had already made his own arrangements for the day. The tourist schedule was light enough for his trawler not to be needed, and he had promised to take a couple of the young lads out deep-sea fishing. Tiffany, of course, was welcome to come along with them, but he warned that the sea was sure to be rough today, and he doubted that they would stay out much longer than midafternoon.

The weather was the least of Tiffany's considerations. However, the presence of the two teenagers made it nigh on impossible for her to make any opportunity for a private chat with Garret. On the way out they wanted him to tell them fishing stories. Then he was busy instructing them on how best to mend, tend and prepare the nets. She didn't really get a moment alone with him. In the end she resigned herself to waiting until they returned home.

Alan called them at lunchtime, anxious about their safety. The barometer was still falling. The wind was up and the sea becoming so choppy that fishing was more of an endurance test than an exciting challenge. Nevertheless, the boys were reluctant to give up until the waves started building to a meter high. Garret called a firm halt then and turned the boat for home. By the time they were nearing Haven Bay, the sea was a formidable height, but the trawler was plowing steadily through it. Tiffany felt no real sense of danger.

The radio crackled with static when Alan came on, wanting to know their position, and then relaying the message that there had been a distress call—a lone sailor from New Zealand, his mast snapped by the wind, his small yacht wallowing helplessly in high seas, taking water too fast for him to cope.

They were all in the wheelhouse. They all heard the details. And they all stared at Garret in shock when he calmly told Alan that the *Southern Cross* could not turn back for a rescue attempt.

"Why aren't we going, Mr McKeogh?" one of the boys asked in bewildered protest, the moment Garret got off the radio.

"We can handle it," the other boy pleaded, appalled at the thought of someone being left to drown.

The old fisherman swung around to face them, his expression as grey and stormy as the waves now crashing across the deck of the trawler. "I'll not be risking three lives for one," he said stonily. "A man who sets out to cross the Tasman Sea alone knows he's taking his life in his hands. That is his responsibility. I brought you out fishing. I bring you safely home. That is my responsibility. I will not answer to anything else."

"But...his boat is sinking!"

"Isn't there some code of the sea?"

Garret visibly bristled at the implied criticism. "Do you forget we have a woman on board?" he demanded, his eyes stabbing briefly at Tiffany before glaring his authority back at the two boys. "We're going home."

Both boys were silenced, but they looked at Tiffany in agonised appeal, not sharing the old fisherman's sense of old-world gallantry that insisted that women should be protected at all costs. Only Tiffany realised that Garret's stance had its roots in a twenty-year-old tragedy, yet she could not condone his decision, either.

"Garret, we must try."

"No! I won't have it!" he declared vehemently.

"I don't want that man's death on my conscience," Tiffany argued. "We have to go. How could we live with ourselves?"

"At least you'll live!" he shot at her. "To turn back now is madness! The seas are high and will start to run a dangerous swell. It will be no fit place for man or beast. Certainly no place for a woman. Why should your life and the life of these two boys be put in jeopardy because a reckless fool has chosen to put his own life at hazard? There will be no more foolishness."

For one unguarded moment there was a glimpse of savage pain in his eyes before he abruptly turned away. The boys looked desperately to Tiffany for more argument, unable to accept Garret's decision. She had a few moments' soul-searching—mostly on the boys' behalf—but she could not feel right about ignoring a distress call even though it did put all their lives in danger.

"Garret, you have no right to make that decision for us," she said quietly. "If it's your own life you're worrying about..."

He threw her a bleakly scornful look. "My life means nothing to me!"

"Then don't use mine as an excuse," Tiffany replied. "I won't wear it, Garret. And neither will the boys. We can't leave that man to die if there's any chance we can save him."

He swept them all with a steely look. He said nothing. His shoulders were rigid as he turned his attention back to the course he was steering. His hands gripped the wheel with white-knuckle intensity. The boat ploughed on. The boys gestured another frantic appeal to Tiffany. She shook her head. There was no way she could force Garret to change his mind, and he was the only one who could handle the trawler in the worsening conditions. The decision was his and his alone now.

The bow of the boat slowly snubbed around and faced into the wind. The boys grinned at Tiffany in relief. She gave them a wry little smile, hoping she hadn't just condemned them all to watery graves. Then she went over to the radio, informed Alan that they were heading out to the lone sailor's last known position and would search for him as long as they could. Garret stared at her in grim-faced silence. The only words he spoke from then on were curt commands, which they all obeyed to the letter.

The next three hours were the most frightening Tiffany had ever spent in her life. The wind increased to gale force, whipping up mountainous seas. Visibility for any distance was utterly impossible. They were no sooner swept up on a huge wave than they were dropped into a deep trough. The trawler creaked and groaned under the constant battering. It was all too clear that they were engaged in a life-and-death struggle with the elements raging around them, yet not one of them suggested they give up and turn back.

It was sheer accident that they found the man at all. One of the boys caught a brief glimpse of the crippled boat and Garret had to use all of his seaman's skills to bring the trawler close enough for a rescue attempt to be made. When he finally positioned the *Southern Cross* some hundred metres downwind from the other craft, he switched all the lights on and ordered the boys to throw a drogue over the side—something similar to an anchor, Garret replied to Tiffany's question. It served to slow down the boat.

"Couldn't we get closer to him?" one of the boys asked.

"Too dangerous! This is the closest we can go without risking a collision. Let's hope the man has wits enough to follow the proper procedure," Garret growled, then gave a grunt of approval as the sailor began hurling drums into the sea.

"Diesel oil," he explained. "The drums have been holed and they'll float towards us, creating an oil slick that will lessen the turbulence of the waves. He should float out a light line attached to a life ring next. Your job—" he eyed the boys with stern authority "—is to hook in that life ring, then haul the man in on the line. The tricky part is lifting him safely aboard without him getting battered to death against the side of the boat."

Nothing proved easy. Only the safety lines that were clipped on to the boys prevented them from being swept overboard a number of times while they tried again and again to pick up the life ring with the all-important line. They were too exhausted to raise a cheer when success was finally achieved. Nevertheless, they hauled in the line with commendable speed, spurred on by the sight of the man at the end of it being drawn closer and closer. The trawler was pitching so much that it was a nightmare getting him safely on board, but they finally managed it. They bundled him below deck. All three of them were soaked through and shivering.

Without a word or look of satisfaction, Garret turned the *Southern Cross* for home. His face might have been carved out of stone for all the reaction he showed to the successful rescue. Tiffany realised that the battle to get them safely back to Haven Bay demanded all his skill and concentration, so she made no attempt at conversation.

For all his years of experience there was nothing Garret could do when they were picked up on a mighty wave. The boat sashayed about, caught in a maelstrom of power. Tiffany heard the propeller come out of the water, heard it start to scream as it wound up its revolutions without the resistance of the water to stop it. A high-pitched whine pierced the howling of the wind. The boat seemed to tremble. Garret cursed and threw the throttle back as the trawler lurched sideways, then skidded off the crest of the boiling inferno of froth into the trough beneath.

It was like falling off the roof of a three-storey building on to the ground below. The force of the impact flung both Tiffany and Garret along the decking and against the stanchions of the wheelhouse. Without their lifelines they would have been washed away. A lesser boat would have broken under the forces, but the *Southern Cross* was Whitton-built to last a century of Antarctic storms.

*We'll all be drowned,* Tiffany thought, her lungs bursting with the need to breathe.

Then slowly, majestically, the groaning creaking timbers of the *Southern Cross* righted themselves and rose above the streaming cascade, high-powered jets of water shooting from the scuppers. Tiffany climbed to her feet in a daze. The wheelhouse was still there, although some of the glasswork had been staved in. She saw Garret stagger upright, his face gashed and unnaturally white.

Her eyes vaguely registered that the radio mast had been snapped. Most of it was gone. Disappeared. The hatch lifted. One of the boys peered out, assuring himself that Garret and Tiffany were still with them, and Garret waved him down again. Tiffany's hands felt numb, but somehow she worked her way back along the line toward Garret.

"Are you all right?" he shouted at her.

"Yes." His face was oozing blood. "I'll get something for your cut," she said.

"There are more serious things than that to attend to," he replied grimly.

"What do you want me to do?"

"We've thrown a propeller blade."

"What does that mean?"

"If we use the engines at any speed we'll pound ourselves to death."

"And if we don't?"

"Then the waves will pound us to death."

"If I don't do something about that cut, you'll bleed to death."

She didn't want to think about Garret's grim forecast. Not yet. One thing at a time, she decided, as she scrambled below deck for a first-aid kit. The boys and the rescued sailor were battered and bruised, but with no bones broken. She did her best to calm their fears,

assured them Garret could still operate the
boat and returned to him with the first-aid
box.

"It's a waste of time," he gruffed at her as
she attempted to dress his face.

Tiffany stubbornly persisted, and finally,
amateurishly, she succeeded in stanching the
bleeding. He stared into her eyes as she did
it, and Tiffany had the eerie sensation that he
was seeing other eyes—eyes that had been the
same azure blue.

"Is the radio still working?" she asked.

He shook his head. "Useless. The aerial is
gone."

She sank on to the bench, shaky now that
she had done all she could do. Garret stood
steadfastly at the wheel, trying to steer them
out of the fatal battering for as long as he
could. They were all going to die, Tiffany
thought, yet that inevitability didn't seem to
have much reality despite her knowing how
desperate the situation was. She wondered if
Joel and Mary-Beth had been unable to believe it could happen to them, that night
twenty years ago. Oddly enough, Tiffany
didn't feel afraid. Somehow she had moved
beyond fear.

"If it was still possible, would you radio for help now, Garret?" she asked curiously.

He didn't look at her. Very slowly he shook his head. "I don't know. I guess I'll never know. I'd hate to risk other lives. For myself, I never would. Maybe for others."

Tiffany pondered that answer for a long time. She did not doubt for a moment that he himself would choose to die rather than endanger other lives. She remembered his furious frustration over the wasted lives in the storm of twenty years ago...lives thrown away against his advice. Yet today he had turned back, against his own code of responsibility.

"There's a remote chance that the navy coastguard might pick us up," he said gruffly. "You can pray for that if you want. Although any detection on radar would be almost impossible under these conditions."

He was offering her a slim thread of hope, but Tiffany knew intuitively that he nursed none at all. He would keep them afloat as long as he could—the old man against the sea that had been his life...and almost certainly his death. Perhaps he even welcomed that end for himself. Was he thinking of the other storm that had ended so many lives?

"I'm sorry for going against you," she said, feeling the weight of responsibility dragging over her. "The boys, they would have backed off if I hadn't pressed it. I just couldn't...."

"Aye, I know," Garret said heavily. "All these years I wished I'd gone after them that night of the storm, suicide or not. I wished I'd gone. It was pride, not fear that stopped me. But it's hard to live with... remembering...thinking what you might have done differently."

"What was Mary-Beth Macauley to you, Garret?" she asked, wanting to know, even though the knowledge was almost certainly useless to her now. "Who was she?"

"My granddaughter."

Tiffany barely heard him above the howl of the wind, his reply was so low, heavy with grief and regret and painful love. The shock of the answer was only momentary. The realisation that there had to have been a close relationship came fast on its heels. It was the link that made everything else understandable.

"Why didn't you stop her from going with Joel in the boat?" she asked softly. "Why blame him for her death?"

He turned bleak empty eyes onto her. "I couldn't stop her. She was going to have a baby... to him."

Tiffany's stomach lurched at the revelation that Mary-Beth had been pregnant by Joel. The shock of it writhed around her mind. They had been so young.

Garret heaved a deep sigh. "I only found out about it that night, the night of the storm. And I was angry. She was little more than a child, my Mary-Beth. I wanted to kill him. I'd trusted him with her and he'd betrayed my trust. God forgive me... I frightened her with the violence of my temper. I was angry with her because she stood up for him, denying that there was anything wrong in what they'd done. It went against everything I believed in."

He shook his head, pain deepening the weathered lines of his face. "I locked her in her room. She escaped somehow. I didn't know she'd got out and gone to him... didn't know she was on that boat until it was under way, and she took off the hood of her oilskins and waved. He had his arm around her, holding her."

"She must have loved him very much," Tiffany commented sadly.

It brought a savage protest. "She was only sixteen! All those childhood years together...as near brother and sister as any siblings...and they made love together!"

"Perhaps that was why the bond they shared was so very close," Tiffany suggested softly. "And the loss even greater for Joel. After all, she was carrying his child. No wonder he became so bitter, so hard and so cynical. He's never got over it, you know. I doubt he ever will."

She paused, then quietly asked, "Can't you forgive him now, Garret? You must know in your heart that Mary-Beth went with him that night because she wanted to, because that was her choice...just as it was my choice a few hours ago not to run for my own personal safety."

He stared back at her without really seeing her, his eyes glazed with pain and memories. Rain lashed the windows. The trawler lurched down another deep trough. The wind shrieked like a thousand lost souls. But it was the storm of twenty years ago that Garret saw and heard.

"He's not the only one to carry the burden of guilt," he said finally, a dreadful hollowness in his voice. "If I hadn't raged at her, she wouldn't have fled to him. She wouldn't have been with him when Reuben insisted on taking out his boat. That's what I've lived with all these years.''

His eyes sharpened on Tiffany's as his voice gathered a thin edge of bitterness. ''But Joel Faber bears the greater guilt. Always will. He shouldn't have let her go with him that night. Just a girl . . . and he knew she was with child. What kind of love is that?''

''Perhaps the kind of love that gives and takes total commitment. Where nothing else matters but being together, sharing whatever comes, for better or for worse.''

Tears blurred her eyes at the thought that she would never know the fulfilment of the hope she had nursed in her heart . . . the hope that she and Joel would share the rest of their lives together. She wondered if Joel would mourn her loss as deeply as he had mourned Mary-Beth's. It did not seem likely. They had known each other such a short time in comparison. And she was not carrying his child.

''If I had been Mary-Beth,'' she said with all the intensity of her own painful emotion, ''nothing in the world would have stopped me from going with him if I thought he might not come back to me. Nothing at all!''

He threw her a sharp look, saw the tears in her eyes and looked away, his face tight and shuttered. He didn't speak again and Tiffany retreated into her own thoughts. She tried not to think of Joel. That was too painful. She summoned up the good memories of life with her family... the fun they had had together... the sharing and the caring... the loving....

One of the boys suddenly burst in on them. "There's a ship bearing north by northeast. About two miles. With our engines running like this—"

"Was it the coastguard?" Garret snapped, scanning the mountainous seas around them.

"No. It was big and white. It could be Mr Faber's yacht, *Liberty*," the boy explained with urgent intensity. "Can we send up flares, Mr McKeogh?"

Garret sliced a look at Tiffany that was strained with conflicting emotions. Her own heart was pounding so hard at the thought that Joel was out there looking for them that she could not begin to appreciate what Garret felt about it.

"Send up the flares," he said curtly. "And start bringing up all the oil drums we've got.

You know what has to be done. We need to be ready.''

The boy raced away to do as he was bidden.

Garret turned towards Tiffany, a poignant mixture of sorrow and curious irony on his face. "So the wheel has turned full circle! Who would have believed it? Yet it's you who's brought him here, isn't it?''

"I hope so,'' she answered fervently. "I hope it's me and not the memory, Garret. However painful that might be for you to hear. But I don't really know. Perhaps he doesn't know, either.''

"It doesn't matter. You are what Mary-Beth might have been if she'd lived. And that doesn't take anything away from you, Tiffany. Never think that. There is no belittlement in having a giving heart. And perhaps, perhaps I've been wrong to blame him. So much ... so totally.''

"Make peace with him, Garret. If you care anything at all for me, please!''

His mouth twisted. "If I get the chance. We'll see. In God's good time, we will see.''

Then the other three joined them. The flares were made ready and fired at paced intervals. It was barely ten minutes later that they sighted the yacht again, bearing straight towards them, and any doubt about its identity was wiped from Tiffany's mind. It was *Liberty*. And this time, Tiffany was quite certain, Joel Faber was intent on getting to her.

# CHAPTER THIRTEEN

"HE'S COME IN too close!" Garret growled.

*Liberty* was a good twenty metres inside the hundred-metre range that Garret considered good seamanship. The huge motor yacht was downwind to the trawler, their relative positions established now by the sea anchor thrown out the back of *Liberty*'s transom.

"He must think it's safe enough," Tiffany offered, although even to her inexpert eye it was only too apparent that in these dangerous seas an extra huge wave could pick up the *Southern Cross* and drive it into the yacht, smashing both craft to smithereens.

Garret swung on her, grey eyes snapping a dismissal of any such contention. "He knows he's being a reckless fool. But I guess we both know what's driving him to take risks. He doesn't want you in that sea any longer than you have to be, Tiffany."

"There are five of us," she protested.

"Joel Faber's not out here for anybody else but you, my girl. He has reason enough never to lift a finger on my behalf. Or for anyone else from Haven Bay. When Mary-Beth died he was made to feel the blame. By all of us. We didn't talk to him, gave him the cold shoulder, completely ostracised him. It was no wonder he left the village. I doubt he will ever forgive us.''

Tiffany couldn't argue with that. She knew Joel hadn't forgiven Haven Bay. And she finally understood the violence of his reaction to her proposition, and why he had never wanted to see her again after that first meeting.

Garret turned away to shout to the boys. ''Start putting the axe into those oil drums, two or three strikes into each, and get them into the sea.''

Tiffany watched them work, denied helping on Garret's command. She knew the old fisherman was just as intent as Joel on not endangering her life any more than he had to. His summary of the situation made her wonder what Joel had thought and felt as he ordered the yacht out into the storm. How deeply had she reached him? Or perhaps the more pertinent question was how deeply was she mixed up with Mary-Beth in his mind?

Joel wanted her in his bed. He had made that clear right from the beginning. Yet there had been something in the way he made love to her last night that suggested he had been seeking more than sexual gratification. So sensitive yet so full of intense yearning. Perhaps needing to recapture what he had once felt so long ago with Mary-Beth...before he had shut himself off from people and become hard and cynical.

He had said that if it could be different with any woman it might be with her. What Tiffany needed to know was how different it had been. And why. What did he feel she gave him— above and beyond all the other women there had been since he left Haven Bay behind? Garret had said that she was what Mary-Beth might have become. Was that what Joel felt about her? Was that why he had been so caring towards her last night?

Then she wondered if any of those things really mattered. She watched the boys hurl out the heavy life ring, and kept her eyes on it as it floated away, taking the line that would link her to Joel once again, if all went well. Garret made them all double-check the fastenings on their life jackets. There was nothing more they could do until the line was secured by the crew on *Liberty*.

''They've got it!'' one of the boys yelled in excited relief.

Garret tied the line around each one of them, carefully spacing the slack in between so that the task of getting them on board *Liberty* would not be complicated by more than one person being lifted out of the water at a time. When they were all secured to his satisfaction, he waited until he judged the most favourable moment, then gave the order to jump.

Tiffany was no sooner in the water than she felt the tug of the line. Whoever was working the *Liberty* end was not wasting any time. She hurtled through oil-slicked waves, grimly holding her breath as the turbulent seas churned her around. Her hair wound around her face. She choked and spluttered every time she managed to get her head above water. She didn't see anything. She didn't even try to look ahead. She just kept gritting her teeth and hanging on to the line with all her strength. She felt the rope hauling her and then she slammed into another body.

She opened her eyes and stared into Joel's face. It was white and strained to a grim gauntness, eyes burning with intense purpose, his mouth biting out words she couldn't hear. His hands gripped under her arms, lifting her past him, using his own body as a cushion to protect hers from being smashed against the boat. Then other hands were reaching for her, dragging her on board. She was swung into a fierce bear hug—Zachary Lee, she thought dazedly—then quickly released to someone else's care.

One of the boys came next. Zachary Lee heaved him on to the deck, and one look at the lad's oil-streaked face gave Tiffany some idea of her own wretched state. But they were alive. A man farther along the deck was holding a TV camera, filming the rescue in the driving wind and rain. The pitching boat made that a hazardous occupation but he stuck at it. Tiffany was frightened to think what Joel was going through. She hadn't seen if there was anything protecting him from being battered against the side of the boat.

The other boy made it safely aboard, then the sailor. There was only old Garret left. And Joel. Tiffany fiercely prayed that nothing would go wrong now. The activity around the winch that was being used on the line seemed to double, extra men stepping in. Her view of what was happening was totally blocked. She pushed her way to the railing, driven by an anxiety too deep to be ignored.

Garret and Joel were being hauled in together. Joel had his arms around the old fisherman, supporting and helping him. Tiffany hoped that Garret might now start to realise how wrong he had been. Joel had cared about everyone. As he had twenty years before. It was not just for her, although she didn't mind that. What he had done, he had done for each of them, with no discrimination at all, and at great risk to himself. Underneath all the hardness and bitterness and cynicism was a good man. A caring man. Hadn't he shown her so on numerous occasions? And to Alan as well.

Tiffany stumbled towards Joel, still entangled in the rope. As if by instinct he swivelled and caught her to him, his arms wrapping around her with crushing strength. He didn't seem to notice that she was an oily, wet, bedraggled mess. He held her so tightly she could feel his heart pounding in his chest as it heaved its anguished relief.

"She's going now!" someone shouted.

They all looked back to see the *Southern Cross* listing farther and farther to one side.

A huge wave crashed over it, driving it to broach in a weird drunken fashion. And then it was as if the sea opened up and swallowed it. Turbulent waves closed over its passing. There was nothing left to mark its grave.

"Sixty years we were together," Garret rasped, bleakly staring at the space where his boat had been.

Joel reached out a hand to grip his arm in sympathy. "I'm sorry we couldn't save it, Garret."

The old man turned and there was agonised sorrow in his eyes. "She lasted twenty years longer than she should have."

In the slashing rain the two antagonists faced each other, neither heeding the external elements that raged around them, as painful memories bound them into a different capsule of time.

"You would have saved her if you could," old Garret said. "I realise that now."

Tiffany intuitively understood that he was not referring to the *Southern Cross,* but to his granddaughter.

Joel's reply came haltingly, strained with agonised doubts. "I've often thought ... wondered ... if there was something I should have done...could have done. If with more foresight...if something was possible..."

Garret brusquely cut in. "I've been wrong all these years, Joel. If it had been at all possible for you to save Mary-Beth, you would have done it. I don't doubt that any more. At the time...you did love her, didn't you?"

"Yes." Joel's arm tightened convulsively around Tiffany. "To me she was all that was good and beautiful. And I couldn't leave her behind that night, Garret. She was too distraught at the thought of being left alone. She wanted to be with me. I had to take her."

"My fault," the old man acknowledged, looking more aged than Tiffany had ever seen him. "I didn't understand. And I'm more sorry than I can say...that things happened as they did."

Joel shook his head. "That night I lost everything that was precious to me. You didn't have to send Tiffany to me to remind me, Garret. I never forgot any of it. When I lost Mary-Beth, nothing mattered any more. Nothing at all. From that day forward, all I did was go through the motions of living...but nothing really meant anything to me."

"It does now," Garret asserted, and the grey eyes turned to Tiffany. "What happened that night..."

"Can happen again," Joel added grimly. "I want you all below and out of this storm. Then I've got to get this boat back to Haven Bay."

They were taken down to the crew's quarters and liberally wrapped in warm blankets. Thermoses of hot coffee laced with brandy were passed around. Joel stayed with Tiffany only long enough to see her rugged up and on the way to full recovery. He ran his fingers lightly over her lips, and the flash of deep hunger in his eyes told her that he didn't want to leave her. But he went, determined to beat this storm and ensure there would be no losses at all this time.

Zachary Lee came and put his arms around her. As her big brother hunkered down beside her, she thought, with considerable irony, that Garret had been wrong about this boat, too. As large as it was, you could certainly feel the sea when it was like this. Zachary Lee had to remove one arm from her to hang on to the side of the bunk she was occupying in order to keep his balance.

"What can I do for you?" he asked in gentle concern. "What do you need?"

She gave him a stiff little smile. "A good scrub and a shampoo in a boiling hot bath. Apart from that, and a few odd bruises, I'm fine."

He nodded. "I guess it's time for me to back down about that guy of yours," he said, his voice gravelling with raw emotion. "He is—" he stopped to clear his throat "—OK."

Tiffany knew that this was about as high an accolade as Zachary Lee would ever give to another man. "I think so," she agreed. "How did he know...?"

"Joel was with me at Q2RV when Alan called. He was worried about you going back out to sea on that search-and-rescue mission after Garret had initially refused to do it. As soon as Joel heard that, he went as white as a sheet. Within seconds he was ordering his yacht on standby and asking for volunteers. Within five minutes we were on our way to it. I don't know how he knew you might be in trouble, Sis, but the way he looked and acted convinced me I had to be with him. Maybe Joel had some sixth sense about it."

Tiffany shook her head. "A long time ago a girl he loved was lost at sea in a storm like this. He's been haunted by it ever since."

Zachary Lee gave her hand a tight squeeze. "That might answer some of it, but I can tell you one thing, Tiff. Joel sure wasn't taking any chances this time. And neither was I."

"You can't fool me," she teased, needing to lighten the choking concern in Zachary Lee's eyes. "You simply came because you wanted your TV interview. And I saw a cameraman filming the rescue, too."

He forced a smile. "Well, now that you mention it, you're right. I'm a media man who will make capital out of anything," he drawled, playing along with her, although they both knew how false that image was. He heaved a deep sigh. "Ruthless, shameless, without feeling for others..."

He seemed lost for words. Tiffany smiled up at this big brother she loved so much. "And a total coward," she supplied helpfully while he was castigating himself.

"Something like that." He smiled back. "But I'm going to get you for that, Sis. You can do the interview now, blanket and all, like it or not."

"Oh, no! Just look at me! I couldn't!"

He grinned. "You look great to me, little sister. Absolutely perfect for a real-life dramatic interview. Besides, it will help pass the time."

He was right about that. It would help distract the others from the storm, as well. "I suppose we could have a go at it," she mused. "Are you going to ask the questions?"

He gave a funny little lopsided smile. "I don't think I've lost the art."

Tiffany considered the position. She wanted Zachary Lee to have his news coup; she wanted to be with Joel even more. "It's a good idea to do the interview now. Once we're back at Haven Bay, Joel and I are going to be together. Alone. No one else. Not for any reason."

Zachary Lee frowned. "Tiff, I was only teasing. It's not that important. I don't expect you to—"

"But we might as well," she argued. "If you want the interview."

He regarded her silently for several moments, then gave her another crooked smile. "I see you've made up your mind again. So I guess we might as well."

It took some time to organise. Tiffany asked for a facecloth to clean herself up a bit, but Zachary Lee refused. He insisted that if she was going before the camera it was better that she look exactly how she was.

''Tell the truth, Sis,'' he reminded her.

Tiffany groaned.

Zachary Lee had not lost the art of making the most of a news report. He took Tiffany through the sea rescue as well as drawing comment about last night's interview with Neil Patterson. He did a masterly job, and when he had wrapped it up Tiffany congratulated him warmly on his professionalism.

He chuckled. ''It's like chess, Tiff...'' He paused, grimaced, then shrugged. ''Just pieces on a board to be moved to the best advantage.''

The shadow of his past was still with Zachary Lee, too, Tiffany thought sadly, as she watched her brother move away to consult with his cameraman.

Was she now irrevocably tied to Mary-Beth in Joel's mind? she wondered. Was that at the root of his ''obsession'' with her? Yet, remembering back to her first meeting with Joel, he had been attracted to her before he noticed the color of her eyes. Attracted enough to offer her a job if she would drop all connection with Haven Bay. And in the end he had been attracted enough to come to Haven Bay for her. He certainly hadn't wanted to lose her.

He might not love her as completely as he had Mary-Beth, but Tiffany could no longer doubt that she meant a lot more to him than a compatible bed companion. They had a future together. Of that she was sure. The only uncertainty was what kind of future they could share. Only when they arrived back at Haven Bay could that even begin to unfold.

The endless pitching and buffeting of the boat seemed to go on forever. Even when *Liberty* entered Haven Bay, the protection from the elements was only relative. The storm was sweeping into it, not over it.

Nevertheless, the atmosphere in the crew's quarters lifted considerably once they were past the cliffs on the headland. The boys began chatting in excited anticipation. They had a great story to tell their families and friends—the adventure of a lifetime. Tiffany's eyes met Garret's. It was a different ending this time, and they were grateful for it, but the shared knowledge of that other ending gave the moment an added poignancy.

She made her way unsteadily over to him, lurching with the pitch of the boat and hampered by the blankets swathed around her. Garret gave her a weary little smile and made room for her beside him.

"Almost there," he said as she sat down.

"Yes. I wanted to thank you."

"No thanks necessary."

"You could have held on to your grievances."

He shook his head. "My only consolation among all my regrets is that my bitter vengefulness backfired on me. I pushed you towards him, Tiffany, with hatred in my heart, not even thinking that you might fill the empty spaces in his life. That's a strange kind of irony, isn't it?"

"Perhaps. It seems to me a lot of things happen in life that you simply can't plan on happening."

"Like your family. That will be good for Joel, too. He only ever had old Reuben, who was more a slave driver than a grandfather."

"He must have had parents somewhere," Tiffany gently prompted, greedy to know all she could about the man she intended spending her life with.

"Not to speak of," Garret said with a grimace. "Joel's mother was a flighty piece. Probably in rebellion to Reuben's hard way with her. She was an unmarried mother and she dumped Joel on Reuben when he was little more than a baby. Ran off with a salesman. Joel was a very lonely unloved boy...except for Mary-Beth.''

''Tell me about her,'' Tiffany urged softly.

A smile of remembrance lit his tired old eyes. ''She was joy and laughter, that child. The light of my life from the moment she came into it. She lived with us from the time she was born and she was everything to me. She was always such a good girl. I guess I spoiled her in most ways, but she never acted spoiled. She was so giving and loving...''

Tears filled his eyes and he shook his head. Tiffany didn't know how to comfort him. ''I'm sorry, Garret,'' she murmured.

''All these years...and she's still so alive to me.''

''There's nothing wrong in keeping the good memories,'' Tiffany said quietly. ''You should always treasure them. They're the gifts of life.''

He patted her hand. ''I hope Joel can give you the happiness you deserve...that Mary-Beth deserved.''

Tiffany hoped she could give Joel that happiness, too. He had had so little loving in his life. No wonder he was hungry for what he had lost with Mary-Beth...living through long joyless years without any expectation of recapturing what had once been his, yet endlessly craving it in the emptiness of his soul.

The engines were throttled right down. One of the crew clattered down the companionway. "We're about to tie up," he announced with a wide grin. "There's a lot of people waiting out there to welcome you home, so if you want to make your way up now we'll get you landed safe and sound." His gaze homed in on Tiffany. "Miss James, Mr Faber said to ask if you'd join him on deck." Then he turned to Zachary Lee. "Mr James, there's transport waiting to take you and your group back to Q2RV."

The exodus was made in as orderly a manner as the conditions allowed. Zachary Lee ended up hoisting Tiffany over his shoulder and carrying her, not letting her down until he delivered her to Joel. "I guess I can trust you to look after her," he said.

"I aim to," Joel replied, hugging Tiffany tightly to his side.

Zachary Lee dropped a kiss on Tiffany's forehead. "Take care. And good luck. And don't get into any more trouble for a while.

I'm going to be awfully busy for quite some time to come.''

"So am I," she returned fervently, then grinned up at him. "Good luck to you, too. Now go and prove you're as good as I said you were."

He laughed and departed.

Tiffany's grin faded as she looked up at Joel. He didn't look quite so grim now, but the strain of the afternoon still showed. His eyes met hers in a dark blaze of need that tore at her heart. "I haven't thanked you," she said huskily.

He lifted his hand and tenderly stroked the ragged strands of hair away from her face. "Will you come with me now, Tiffany?" he asked, a raw edge of emotion rasping through every word.

"Yes. I'll do whatever you want, Joel," she answered simply. Then because she wanted to give him everything he might want from her, she added, "I love you."

And she reached up and brought his head down to hers, kissing him without a care in the world for what anyone else might think, because only what Joel thought and felt mattered to her at that moment, and she wanted him to feel her love, know it and realise it was his for the taking.

There was a brief hesitation on his part, as though he wasn't sure how to respond, but then his arms closed possessively around her, claiming her as his, and his mouth moved over hers in sweet yearning hunger, savouring the totality of her gift to him, making her feel both infinitely cherished and infinitely wanted.

A horribly familiar and strident voice broke in on them. "I've got you this time, Joel!" Nerida Bellamy declared with gloating triumph, and as Tiffany opened her eyes she was almost blinded by a flashlight.

"Yes, Nerida. You've got me," Joel agreed, and he didn't sound the least bit unhappy about it.

"You can't deny there's a love interest now," Nerida crowed.

"I'll even give you an announcement," Joel conceded. "I intend to marry Miss James as soon as we can get her whole family together for the wedding—all of her brothers and sisters, along with her remarkable parents. And now, if you'll excuse us, one of Miss James's sisters and a nephew are waiting for us."

"In the meantime, and until the wedding, we will publish," Nerida declared, obviously threatening that nothing Joel could do would stop her this time.

"Publish and be damned!" Joel tossed back at her. "What do I care? I'm going to be married."

He swept Tiffany between the newspaper reporter and her photographer and headed for the gangway. Tiffany made no protest. Her head was whirling ecstatically with the idea of her and Joel's wedding...if he really meant it. She didn't even feel the wind and rain as Joel hurried her along the wharf, and didn't notice the crowd of people clustered at the stone wall until they reached it.

The fathers of the rescued boys wanted to shake Joel's hand and express their gratitude. He responded stiffly, ill at ease with being the focus of approval in this village. He broke away from them as quickly as he could, using Tiffany as the obvious excuse.

The red Bentley was parked nearby and Payton was waiting beside the passenger door. "Joel, we can't get in the Bentley like this!" Tiffany protested. "We'll ruin it!"

"Not to worry, miss. I spread out a couple of rugs," Payton assured her. "It's good to see you back with us, miss," he added with a wide grin.

"Turn around," said Joel, "and look at Haven Bay. Take it all in, Tiffany. Just as it is now. An old fishing village. Imprint a memory of it that will last the rest of your life."

She knew what he meant, of course. She was going with Joel and he would never come back. Even though some wounds had healed, he would never find any joy in this place. He had come back for her, but now that necessity was past.

She did as she was bidden, the blanket wound tightly around her shoulders. Unlike Joel, she loved every aspect of Haven Bay, the row of old-fashioned shops facing the harbor, the cobblestoned paving around the solid stone wall, the sweeping curve of the bay....

The realisation of what had happened came as a heart-wrenching, mind-jolting shock. "Oh, my God!" she cried, automatically clutching at Joel in her distress.

"What's wrong?"

"They aren't out there! They're gone!" She looked up at Joel in despairing helplessness. "You said it would happen."

He searched the area in incomprehension before stabbing his gaze down at her in anxious concern. "What's happened?"

"The whales! The humpback whales! The storm has driven them away from Haven Bay!"

# CHAPTER FOURTEEN

TIFFANY WAS RENT by conflicting emotions as Joel bundled her into the car. She had to go with him. Her happiness and his depended on it. Yet with the whales gone from Haven Bay, what would happen to the fledgeling tourist industry? Alan's and Carol's future depended on it! And there were all the others she had encouraged to invest their time and money. If it all collapsed now, it would be exactly the disaster that Joel had predicted.

Why did this storm have to happen at just the wrong time, before everything was really established? In another few years it wouldn't have mattered so much. They would have had other things going for them. On the other hand, if the storm hadn't happened, where would she be in her relationship with Joel?

"Tiffany."

Reluctantly she turned up her gaze to meet Joel's, unable to hide her inner agonising. She loved him so much, but this was not something she could share with him. He wasn't interested in Haven Bay. He had warned her against going ahead. Why did she always think she could do these things? That everything would work out right if she just put enough effort into it?

Joel put his arm around her and lifted his other hand to her cheek in soothing reassurance. "It will be all right," he said. "I've taken care of the future here, whales or no whales. But they will come back, Tiffany. It might be a few days, a week or two, even longer, but Haven Bay will survive. And prosper. I promise you that."

Tiffany's mind whirled again. "What do you mean, you've taken care of the future here?" she asked in bewilderment.

She couldn't grasp any sense at all out of what he'd said, yet his eyes were telling her he cared about what she felt, and promising her that nothing bad was going to happen. And then he smiled, completely neutralising the conflict inside her and injecting a warmth that grew and grew as he explained.

"While you were giving me a rise in ratings at Q2RV, I was setting up a deal with the shire council for a comprehensive tourist development here at Haven Bay. The plans are about to be approved. That's why I told you to take in what it's like now, Tiffany. In a few months it won't be the same...ever again."

"You did that for me, Joel?" she choked out, overwhelmed by such a flood of emotion she could barely speak. It was almost unbelievable that he had turned completely around in his thinking.

"There aren't many people like you," he replied softly. "People who do things for others without expecting or demanding any reward or recognition for it. I need you in my life, Tiffany. Whatever I had to do to get you, I was determined to do. I didn't really care if you failed at Q2RV. The fact that you were trying to succeed for me, meant more to me than any success. And I knew how I was going to cover you if you did fail. But Haven Bay was still a barrier. I could see that if your initiatives for this old village failed it would become a problem between us. And it would hurt people you cared about. People like Alan and your sister, who didn't deserve any more hurt. And the others who wanted some future here."

"So you decided to throw in your backing after all, even against your own judgement and inclination," she said, awed that one act of giving on her part had had so deep an effect on him.

He winced at her words. "You were right when you said I was unfairly prejudiced against the place."

"No, I wasn't right," she denied swiftly, all too aware that he was the one who had suffered unfair prejudice. "I didn't know what had happened to you here. Not until today when we thought we wouldn't get back, and Garret finally told me all of it." She searched his eyes anxiously. "You don't mind any more?"

"Not if I have you," he answered simply. And there was no pain in his eyes at all, only a deep, deep hunger for her and for the future that could be theirs together.

"You'll always have me," she promised, a sweet relief rushing through her at the realisation that the loss of Mary-Beth had finally been put to rest. She flung her arms around his neck and nestled her body against his, her eyes shining up at him with unbridled love.

His face relaxed into another smile. "Then you will marry me?" he asked.

She laughed and kissed him, almost bursting with happiness. "Only if you insist."

Her eyes danced teasingly. "And you have to do that, because Nerida's going to publish."

Laughter bubbled out of his throat, and she stared up at him in joyous wonder. It was the first time she had ever heard him really laugh from the heart; the first time she had seen his eyes glow with a deep inner pleasure. And he didn't look so hungry anymore. The strain, the tension, the ever-wary watching, the hardness, the cynicism...they had all been swallowed up in that short burst of laughter. She silently vowed to make him laugh a lot more in future, to put as much joy as she could into his life.

And she would give him a baby. Lots of them. They would have a big family. And they would be so happy together. And she would get rid of the security guards at Leisure Island so that their home would not be a fortress that shut out the rest of the world. It would become a playground for their children, full of joyous laughter. And life would be so worth living, so rich with the things that were worth living for.

She looked up and found Joel's eyes resting on her, his brows drawn together in slight puzzlement. "Is everything all right?" he asked, his tone lightly edged with concern.

She smiled away his concern. "How could it not be? You keep covering me at every turn, making sure everything's all right."

"I need you to show the way," he said, his eyes darkening with intense emotion. "I always will, Tiffany. Without you..."

"I need you, too, Joel," she said quickly, stroking his cheek in loving reassurance. "We were meant to come together. I felt that when I first met you, and I feel it even more strongly now. There's no parting for us. Ever."

"Tiffany." He released a long shuddering breath, not even realising he had been holding it as she promised him the life he had thought could never be his. He felt almost dazed with disbelief that this was really happening, that she could love him as she did. But it was there in her eyes, in her voice, in every word she spoke.

"Kiss me, Joel," she pleaded softly. "Kiss me with all the love in your heart. With all the love that is ours in the future."

He did not hear the rain lashing the car windows. He did not hear the lonely howl of the wind outside. He did not see Payton turn the rear-vision mirror aside. There was no one else in the world. Only her. There was no storm. Only the most blissful peace. And he held her tightly to his heart and kissed her with love—a love that filled his soul and poured into hers in a never-ending stream.

A journey of a thousand miles, he thought, begins with a single step. And already he had come a long way. He knew how much he had changed, how much Tiffany had already given him. He vowed to keep following her lead, to take every step she showed him. Wherever she went he would go, eternally grateful to be with her.

Life was so worth living now. It did have meaning. It would always have meaning... with Tiffany.